My Mind's Café

28 Stories for a Love Tooth

Juju's Pearls

INDIA • SINGAPORE • MALAYSIA

Everything starts from a seed of thought.

Healthy, positive seeds of thoughts are the key to a happy, fun-filled, enriched, life.

Love adds the much-needed magical aroma.

Life is all about making memories.

Make sure you create a beautiful one.

You are a source of inspiration for those around you.

Keep believing, keep inspiring!

ALSO BY JUJU'S PEARLS

Momsie Popsie Diary Tea-Time Chit-chat on Living Life

Other books/anthologies:

#Verses of love

Love Me, Till Your Cessation!

My Feelings on the Paper Book 1 of My Heart Goes On

Wide Awake Volume 1

How I Calibrate My Life!

The Kolkata Diaries Volume II

Summer Waves Volume II

Stories from India Volume I

Heartfelt thanks,

To my life lines —Neelesh, Savika and Aaditya.

Seeking blessings from my Momsie (Mrs Kailash Goel) and Popsie (Shri Gopal Das Goel), who are my inspiration and add a magical essence to all my writings.

I dedicate this work to every living soul on this Mother Earth who has touched my life and helped me in evolving as a compassionate, caring, loving, complete, human being.

I am a continuous work in progress!

Dedicated to all,

Teachers and friends from Cambridge School, New Delhi

MBBS teachers and friends from Bangalore,

Teachers and friends from TMH (Tata Memorial Hospital), Mumbai

Each phase of my life has been beautiful,

I owe them.

CONTENTS

HOW TO READ THIS BOOK—MY SUGGESTION

This is an attempt to explore love in various dimensions as a collection of stories encompassing elements of love.

Love is an emotion, an experience with anyone and anything. Besides, the usual love between parents and their children and man-woman, love is multi-dimensional and way beyond our thoughts. It cannot be calibrated and follows no rules. Love follows the heart.

So, I request my readers to go through this book with an open mind. Some concepts of love may touch a deep chord whereas others might make you sceptical. One may feel it's his or her own story, at another point, it might be a story about someone you know. Just go with the flow and read it like a story of life. The best part is you can begin reading from any page and leave it on any page.

As one goes by the various contents, one may feel the intensity and maturity reaching a higher orbit. At times very smoothly and insidiously and at times without any word of caution, just like a freshly brewed cup of tea/coffee. So, just sit back, and read by with a cup of morning tea/coffee and enjoy the brews from *My Mind's Café*.

Pure bliss for the soul!

Disclaimer

This is a work of fiction. Unless otherwise indicated, all the names, characters, businesses, places, events and incidents in this book are either the product of the author's imagination or used in a fictitious manner to relate real-life anecdotes as stories. Any resemblance to actual persons, living or dead, or actual events is purely coincidental.

The author has tried to cover only some aspects of love that have touched her in the form of stories. It will require another lifetime to understand love and its dimensions entirely.

BOOK JOURNEY

As I was about to finalise publishing my book, I received a message from my alma mater group. One of my friends had lost her father in the wee hours of the morning. The kind of emotion and love that created a whirlpool in my heart, led me to think, "I have missed writing a story about this wonderful, pure love between two friends, my hostel roommate. It's been such a weird twist of destiny that four of my buddies lost their fathers within a short time of six months."

I always extend my support with the statement, "Don't worry! My Momsie will take care of your loved one. She is very close to God and knows the ways of the other world way too well."

To my family and children, I always joke, "Now, we have a direct approach with God." This helps ease the pain and grieving lips curve into a smile.

Hope each reader relates to these stories in one way or another.

Wishing you a happy, blissful reading journey in the magical world of books!

PROEM

18th June holds a special place in my heart as I experienced my first love and first sorrow, though in different timelines. Twenty-three years ago, I boarded the Mumbai-Delhi-bound train, Rajdhani Express, to meet the love of my life. My tryst with love started on this date.

Seven years ago, a routine visit to my hometown, New Delhi during summer vacations changed my life forever. On 18th June 2015, Thursday, my mother left her mortal coil in my lap. A part of me went in her pyre. This was my tryst with grief. It took me nearly five years for closure. I am not really sure about it. But yes, now when I speak about my Momsie my tears don't roll down my cheek and my voice doesn't quiver. I share my experiences with those who have lost their loved ones.

I am always available for them if they need a listening ear and at times for a counselling session. My workplace is an open place for such discussions. Unburden# unload your grief and fill your emotional saucer with love and positivity.

I realised, "A lot could happen over tea too!"

Love is a strong emotion. Mother-child love is the purest form of love. There are many unexplored dimensions. So, here we set out to explore. Where love goes, happiness flows.

> *"Helping others heal is a path to self-healing."*
>
> — Juju's Pearls

ACKNOWLEDGEMENTS

With a heart full of gratitude and love, I wish to acknowledge every person who touched my life over the last four decades. A human being is a summation of his genetic make-up and surroundings. I have been blessed to have such wonderful, inspiring people in my life.

All my friends, my readers and my colleagues, besides my family, have stood by me and helped me in polishing my writing skills and never doubted me. This helped me in experimenting with a different genre. They are my continuous source of inspiration.

I believe in 'A*spire to* I*nspire*'.

1

LAVENDER LOVE

Unconditional Love!

God has bestowed us with a wonderful sensory system. All the five senses play a pivotal role in our lives and are connected with our emotions and certain situations, in happiness and sadness both. Sharon was a preterm baby. Her mother delivered her during her seventh month of pregnancy. She stayed in the neonatal intensive care unit for two months and was discharged once she weighed two kilograms. She was born after a gap of twenty years of marriage. So, in this way she was a special child. Her mother was devoted and gave up her job to raise her. Her mother wore a particular lavender fragrance and Sharon used to find warmth and security in that smell. She felt her mother's presence nearby. Gradually she gained strength and was at par with children of her age. After completing her schooling, she enrolled in a university across the other coast of the country. After graduation and her master's, she joined a doctorate programme. Contact with her parents decreased as she was riding the uphill of success and her parents were treading downhill in the journey of life.

Sharon started enjoying her life and gradually started drifting towards the ills of society. Once she was arrested for driving while drinking too. On her parent's golden jubilee anniversary celebrations, she celebrated with full enthusiasm, seeking forgiveness for her irresponsible behaviour. With a promise to be in regular touch, she flew back. Her parents were overjoyed by her mere presence and did not disclose the terminal-stage cancer her mother was fighting. Her mother's deteriorating health troubled her father, and he called up Sharon. After unsuccessful attempts, he left a voice mail message to contact him immediately. His wait stretched into weeks and one day his wife got defeated in the fight with cancer. He was devastated and full of remorse. After so much difficulty, his wife had given birth to Sharon, their only child, and his wife died waiting for her. Honouring the promise made to his wife, he sent a message to Sharon to come home by the very next flight.

His wife had taken the promise that her body would be buried only after Sharon arrives. The whole house should smell of her favourite, lavender, no one should break this sad news to Sharon until she arrives and sees for herself. Sharon called back and informed him about her travel plans. When she reached her hometown, she felt a feeling of anguish and sadness. The driver was waiting for her. With head bowed, he kept her luggage and silently drove towards their home. Sharon's attempts to break the silence failed. As she reached her porch, she saw a swarm of people with sad expressions. Her heart pumped louder and louder. Slowly, she opened the main door; the same lavender fragrance hit her. This had a calming effect for she was relieved that her mother was nearby. She felt the same security and comfort as she had felt in her childhood. Paving the way amongst relatives, her eyes searched for her parents, especially her father. Inwardly, she was feared the worst. Suddenly, she saw her father in a sombre mood in one corner. She hugged him from behind and almost yelled, "Dad, where is Mom?" Her father turned his face towards his left side and pointed the index finger of his right hand towards the lawn. Sharon rushed outside.

The lawn scene swept the ground underneath her feet. She saw a glass chamber coffin. A woman in a bridal dress was inside in a sleeping posture. Her feet seemed to stick to the ground. With great effort, she inched her foot one by one towards the coffin. There were lavender plants everywhere—English and French varieties—her mother's favourite. Inside, she knew what she was going to see. She ran towards the chamber and slid the cover open. There, inside the chamber, her mother was lying in a peaceful pose with a piece of paper in her hand.

Suddenly, she felt a hand on her left shoulder. She turned and hugged her father. All the while she was running around making a life for herself that she forgot her parents were growing old and they might need her. A feeling of remorse and bitterness engulfed her and she started weeping loudly. Her father comforted her and asked her to read the last letter from her mother. With trembling hands, she opened it. Her mother had written a beautiful paragraph for her.

Dear Sharon,

We waited for twenty long years before God blessed us with you. With your birth, I felt complete and it gave me a purpose in life. Our lives revolved around you. We know you were embarrassed at times during your parent-teacher meetings because we looked older than other young parents. We always wanted you to have a flight of your own and build a nest wherever you wanted to. In this process, I forgot to mention that when a bird flies away, she knows about her nest and where to come back. Your nest is in our arms, our house where you grew up. Every nook and corner has a story to tell.

I stopped your father from letting you know about my terminal-stage cancer when you visited us on our golden jubilee anniversary. I always wanted to leave this world with your smiling face as my memory. Please forgive your father. He was honouring my promise.

I got lavender plants planted on our lawn so that whenever you come home to visit your father, you should always feel me. Please forgive me for hiding my illness. I love you my darling daughter for you made my life worth living. God always bless you,

Love,

Mom

Sharon read the letter umpteen times, sat with the plants, and touched them with her finger. She felt connected as if her mother had left her mortal coil only. Her mother was everywhere in this fragrance. It was time to bury her mother. She walked with her father and laid her mother's coffin to rest. With her father, they planted lavender plants near the grave with a message:

'Laid to rest only in physical form, her fragrance spreads in all directions.

Love, Sharon and Dad'

After the church ceremony, she went back to the west coast. She shifted her base to her hometown and started living with her father. Having tea together on the lawn with lavender fragrance in the morning air entering their nose reminds her that her mother is nearby and giving them company.

2

MUST HAVE BEEN LOVE!

Innocent Love

In a corner of a country, a boy was born after three girls in an affluent family. It was a festive feel in the entire village. Month-long celebrations went on and none of the households in the entire village cooked any meals for a month. This blue-eyed boy, Jared was everyone's favourite. He was brought up with a lot of love and pampering by his parents and sisters. He was not used to the word 'no' being said to him as everything was in the affirmative as far as he was concerned. Years rolled by and the time came to leave the nest. He was an average student in academics but excelled in sports. This helped him secure admission to one of the country's reputed colleges.

It was his first day in college. Jared's heart skipped a beat and he experienced butterflies in his stomach when he saw a beautiful girl with long hair, holding books in her hands crossed against her chest, coming towards him. She seemed like a fresher just like him. She asked him very politely, "Please help me in finding the lecture hall for the first year." Jared could not control his excitement. Trying to keep himself calm and composed, he just guided her in the wrong direction.

Later in the lecture hall, his eyes kept searching for the girl. After the lunch break, he saw the girl in the hall with red, swollen eyes. He mustered courage and walked up to her. Immediately, she looked up and spoke, "Please let me know the real reason why you misguided me. I entered the final year lecture hall and was ragged. You have hurt me a lot. I missed my first two lectures because of you." She sounded sad and left without a word.

Jared felt deeply hurt. The girl who had stirred some different feelings in him was angry with him. He befriended her best friend to get to know her and to apologise to her. He came to know that Jas came from an educated family and was a topper in her state. Jas was very clear in her goal in life. Jared sent her sorry notes, flowers and chocolates. Jas was oblivious of Jared's feelings towards him. So, she assumed them to be for her friend Lim, as she had seen Jared and Lim together a few times in the cafeteria. The flowers and cakes kept coming regularly. Both Jas and Lim thought it was for the other one.

Finally, one day, both decided to talk about it openly. Jas told Lim, "Jared was not as good as he looked. She felt he was stalking her, though he was committed to Lim." Hearing this, Lim burst into laughter, in disbelief and spoke, "Jas, how could you ever think like this? Right from day one in college, ever since Jared saw you, he knew you were the one." She continued, "Jared was just seeking my help in delivering the flowers and the chocolates. Now I see why you never touched them. Hope you must have read his sorry notes which were addressed to you?"

At this point, Jas was in tears, and she hurriedly went inside the room to search for sorry notes. All the sorry notes were addressed to her. Almost, like a flash of lightning, everything became clear to her. All this while, Jared had his eyes only for her. She misunderstood him as she had seen him with Lim a few times, sipping coffee together. Deep inside, she had liked him a lot and was jealous of Lim.

Lim arranged a date for both of them. When they met, only their eyes made contact and all the vows were exchanged. They both realised what true love actually felt like.

3

TRUE LOVE!

Soul Love

In this infinite world, there are 99% things that a human mind doesn't know, that it cannot know. Yet, whenever promises are made, the mind wants an eternal promise. Although the heart knows it's unrealistic, for a loving soul it is a sign of true love and commitment.

A young doctor comes to a tertiary care hospital for a job interview. As she walks towards the lift to press the button, out of nowhere a figure in blue and white appears in front of her and enters the lift in a hurry. All she hears is, "Sorry", and a big generous smile on his face. Her heart skips a beat, she stands frozen. She sees a twinkle in the boy's eye as the lift ascends, or it was just her imagination? She decides to take the staircase and go to the administrative block. She gets the job with immediate joining.

God had some surprises in store for her. It turns out the boy in the lift is her immediate boss. Hiding their feelings, they work as the best team. Both are of a slender frame with good looks and intelligent minds. When they are together, everything seems perfect and just right. All this while, it has always been a professional, work-related talk. The air in between them is always charged and vibrant. No words are ever said, only glances exchanged. Anyone can vouch that their relationship seems like a promise of eternity.

Gathering courage, he invites her for lunch. When they are together, words seem to vanish, and only their souls talk. He spills the beans and says, "Do you have feelings for me?" Taken aback by the straightforward question, she keeps quiet.

Sensing her discomfort, he continues, "I noticed you on the very first day when you walked towards the lift. Your blue dress, black tresses tied up, your gentle smile and confident, graceful walk. Ever since then, I prayed to God that you should be the recruit. I feel you are the one for me and we are meant to be together."

He takes a pause, breathes deeply, and continues, "I committed to a girl just two months ago. Now I feel uneasy as I can see my future right in front of my eyes, but my commitment holds me back. Please help me."

They eat their lunch in complete silence. On their way back, in the car, he puts on their favourite music and waits. She looks at him and smiles (the most beautiful, loving smile ever), "I appreciate your honesty and can understand your situation. Love just happens! This is one emotion that looks beyond colour, caste, creed, status, etc. You are committed, that is what the truth is."

He feels uneasy, "It is important for me to know whether you like me or not?" She smiles and replies, "What do you feel? Do I need to answer?"

At that moment something magical happens as if the divine intervenes to help these beautiful souls. He says, "I will love you till my last breath and beyond." She smiles in agreement and softly says, "I do."

Promises are exchanged for life and beyond. This memory remains as fresh as a flower in their hearts to date and their love is beyond their last cessation.

4

LOVE THY SELF

For Dust You Are, Into Dust, You Shall Return!

What is life? This thought is intriguing to many, especially to me, which leads to introspection. Life is a divine gift that must be utilised well in a fulfilling, satisfying manner. There should not be any space for any regret when we are at the twilight of our journey. If we consider life as a dimension, then we can think of calibrating it too. The beauty is that life always happens at the moment, life happens now.

So, let's calibrate now. Each one has the power to introspect oneself and can calibrate it too. The aim is to live a pure, peaceful, powerful, contented and happy life. Calibration rules can be laid down as per the different spheres of one's life. Like in terms of physical health, mental, emotional, social, financial, spiritual, etc. to name a few major areas. Depending upon our priority, one can alter/shift the calibration on the scale. More or less, the parameters are the same for everyone with a few modifications on a one-to-one basis.

A simple way to improve physical health is by adopting a healthy lifestyle. Regular exercise and a balanced diet are the key. This is easier said than done. One can create support groups with the same motive of staying healthy. There are numerous morning walker clubs, cycling clubs, marathon runners' clubs, etc. Enrolling in your local gym or yoga classes is another option.

Simple choices such as using the staircase instead of the lift or walking to the local market are little subtle changes in one's lifestyle that promise long-term health benefits. Engaging in a sports activity—be it outside or inside, is another very good option in many cases. Once a week, have a small health awareness talk by an expert. Enrol in annual health check-ups to get the actual results. The mantra is 'Just move'. If space is not a constraint, then taking up gardening as a hobby or growing one's vegetable garden is another excellent initiative.

We are a by-product of our surroundings. It is of utmost importance that our mental state is calibrated and synchronised. The company we keep influences our personality. Mental energy is the powerhouse that determines our entire functioning. What we see and what we hear leads to how we process things and what we convey. One should be wary of what goes on in one's brain. The information must be positive and must always carry food for thought. There is a general predisposition towards negative news. The mind tends to believe negative news very easily, even without verifying it. Whereas, positive news needs to undergo many rounds of verification. Keep your mental status secure. Surround yourself with motivated, sincere, hardworking people from the human race. You are known by the company you keep. So be careful and choose your circle wisely.

Emotion is an abstract state. Calibration is very difficult, yet not impossible. Emotions can be classified as soft and hard. One needs to identify their emotional behaviour and responses throughout the day, week and month. There are certain triggering situations. Such types of recurring emotions can be dealt with in a graded manner. One is usually aware of the kind of emotions that will surface in certain situations. One must learn to identify such situations. That moment of consciousness leads to a proactive response rather than a reaction.

Always remind yourself, "Anyone or anything that robs you of your mental peace is just not worth it." Meditation and silence are important tools to empower oneself to control and liberate emotions at one's own slow pace. Calibration in this area is most challenging and requires continuous reinforcement, time and again. The fact is that it is an ongoing process till our last breath.

"Man is a social animal." To celebrate we need company. Hence, your social circle plays a very crucial role in your overall development and personality. Keep your circle limited to avoid unnecessary troubles. The smaller the circle is, the lesser are the confrontations and problematic situations. In defining ways to calibrate one's social life, first and foremost there should be complete acceptance of oneself. Don't imitate others or do things just to impress or fit in any particular kind of group. Each one is unique. What suits one person, may not go well with the other one. This doesn't mean you don't fit. Learn to know your limits. Define your do-s and don't-s. Be comfortable with your good self and learn when to say 'no'. Everyone likes an easy-going, good-natured person who doesn't judge. Calibrate points of being non-judgemental and comfortable in your skin as on top of the list.

We earn to make our lives comfortable, and not miserable. Unfortunately, many of us, in the zest to earn money forget the very basis of it. Tools to calibrate your financial sphere are many. Whatever may be the nature of one's work and income generated, one must practice the formula of 40-30-30 to lead a financially stable life. 40% of income goes for paying bills, taxes, and other daily running expenses. 30% of it must be utilised on oneself and family to experience the beauty of life. The remaining 30% should be saved for adverse situations. Many a times this formula can be 50-30-20 or some other combination. It is important to have a two-digit figure in all three places.

One can seek help from financial advisers too. Sound financial health is a great morale booster and is the big key to your mental and emotional health.

The latest craze in the twenty-first century is 'spiritualism', which in reality is as old as early civilisation. Awareness of being in the moment is the simplest tool to become spiritual. Recognising your native core nature is the goal of spiritual awakening. The best way is to introspect, understand and be one's own self. To be able to do this, one has to confront one's own worst fears. It's always easy to find fault in others and very difficult to find one's own shortcomings. Whatever way one decides to choose, be it by following a teacher or by doing it by oneself, it is important to be true to oneself.

The concept of calibrating life is a very interesting but still unexplored dimension. My take is to live life as it comes. Define your own line and go with the flow. Life is lived best by those who just simply live it and at times is messed by those who analyse it too much. Life is just 1% that happens and 99% how you make it. Enjoy this beautiful blessing by God and repeat, "I am living a miracle called life."

5

CIRCLE OF LIFE!

Origin of Love

Prologue

This story doesn't revolve around a character who is a superwoman or downtrodden or a woman who has been physically abused or is physically disabled etc.

This story is our story, the story of every female who takes birth on this planet. This is about the daily challenges, small or big, which she faces right from the time she is born, her different growth stages, her school life, college life, workplace, and marriage—pre and post.

If one is honest about their individual experiences and shares them in the same spirit without adding on, I believe this world would be a better place. The stigma of being judged is so deeply rooted that most women don't come out in the open to talk about the abuse, be it verbal, physical, mental, social or professional.

Our society is male-dominated, and females have often been portrayed as objects of desire and want. Very less is talked about their individuality or their personality. They are considered subordinate to the male species of their kind, the highest evolved species on Mother Earth. The world smells of hypocrisy.

Women are worshipped during the day and the scenario changes as the day dawns.

A majority of us will resonate with this story.

It's about us, our journey.

Story

Woman, the finest creation of God, seems like God made her from the soul. Yet, human beings tend to question the Almighty by suppressing and oppressing her. The physical attributes and emotional bent of a woman have led to the creation of a wide gap. In the game of power play, the one with superior physical strength wins. Maybe this has led to terms like the weaker sex, the fairer sex, women empowerment, and so on.

The whole concept of women-empowerment seems hypocritical. First, you label women as less powerful and then play the philanthropic role of women empowerment. Who has given man the right to question creation? As such, it's more important for a woman to empower another woman. Then we don't need to rely on anyone. For ages, a woman has been the toughest opponent of another woman. One can go down the pages of history to verify this. A woman assumes various roles in a lifetime and is engulfed with insecurities in different decades of her life. As a child, she has to strive for attention from her parents and society at large to be able to get recognition as a living being. The next decade brings about physical changes and she struggles with the transition from a child to an adolescent. Further decades escalate to youth, womanhood, and the associated responsibilities. All along she has women in her circle adorning different roles as mothers, sisters, grandmothers, teachers, friends, house helpers, etc. Unknowingly, their impact leaves a footprint in her memory. She becomes a summation of many such footprints and these are her shields in challenging times.

Let's understand this by going through the story of one such XX genotype Joa, who stood the test of time and emerged as a winner. She shut the mouths of society and persons in her family. Joa is a normal girl who did ordinary things in extraordinary ways, which polished her and she turned into a priceless diamond. Each stage of her life is filled with stories of her courage, strength, and ability to consider problems as situations and setbacks as opportunities.

The initial decade since Joa opened her eyes first was a smooth ride. As she entered her teens, she felt that the world around her had changed. Everyone started looking at her like an object. She could feel the infinite piercing eyes, which scanned her from top to bottom, left to right. She started feeling vulnerable. She had a great relationship with her parents and she shared her fears. Her mother counselled her regarding the phase of entering her teens and the physical changes that begin to occur in girls. Since the growing girl becomes conscious of these changes, the feeling of being watched and judged comes as part of the packaged deal. Furthermore, her mother suggested that she enrol in self-defence classes and join some sports activities that will make her physically strong and will help in alleviating these thoughts. Joa felt relieved and joined hockey and self-defence classes. While going from home to school or for classes, holding a hockey stick in her hand, she felt empowered from within. She gained self-confidence that she was armed and ready to face the world.

One day while going home by public transport, she didn't get a seat. As a result, the obvious choice was to stand with some support. After a while, she felt something hard pressing behind her. She felt pressure and moved forward just when the bus took a turn and the pressure from behind came with much stronger force. She looked behind a saw an elderly, bald man who winked and smiled at her. In the flash of a second, she realised what the man was thinking. He was having a hard-on, and taking advantage of the situation, was deriving dirty pleasure. She pulled her hockey stick out and thumped on the ground intending to hit the man. It worked, her stop came and she alighted from the bus.

She learnt that if a girl greets or smiles at co-passengers, society views it as an invitation. She narrated the incident to her mother. Her mother advised her to be bold, enough to tackle the situation she might be in. If she is in a crowd, she could think of giving it back. On the other hand, if she was alone, the best approach would be to ignore the situation and try to reach a safer place. That day, some strange power seemed to seep inside her that made her strong.

College life was a roller coaster ride too. But she viewed problems as challenges and converted them into opportunities. She had to wear glasses in college due to myopia. Most of the boys used to make fun of her and made comments like, "Oh! You have four eyes, so you must be possessing extra clear vision now." Once, while on a college trekking trip, one of the seniors who was involved with her roommate tried to take advantage of her. She shared this with her roommate and convinced her to leave him and move ahead in life. Respecting and maintaining the dignity of her colleagues became a priority.

No wonder she was chosen as the President of her college. This position brought her in contact with youth politicians. This moment changed her life forever. After winning the President's post, she was coaxed into throwing a party for her supporters. Little did she know, this was a game plan of her senior, the same who had misbehaved on the college trip. He was the son of a famous politician who had never heard the two-lettered word 'no' in his life. His ego had been bruised and he was hell-bent on destroying Joa.

At the party, there was music and drink cocktails were being served. The party was going well past midnight when the trance was broken by the screeching sound of police cars. In a matter of a few minutes, the party scene metamorphosed into a crime scene. Police had a tip and had come with a search warrant. On investigation, drugs were found and Joa got arrested. She was the host and was responsible for what was being served that evening. Her cries of pleading, "Not guilty" fell on deaf ears. At this point, her father stepped in to support her. He hired the best lawyers and she was absolved of all charges. One of her friends gave testimony that the drugs were brought by the politician's son. Her father advised her not to press charges against the boy. That day she reaffirmed that she will be very careful in treading her path and will not blindly believe anyone. That night she had a long talk with her father about the ways and behaviour of the male species.

She was slightly overweight and her physical appearance brought about many rejections at job interviews. The majority of firms wanted typically stereotyped females as shown in magazines, in a body-conscious state. What was expected was a female candidate with a slender frame, wearing smart dresses and footwear with appropriate makeup and hairdo. It was all about the exterior appearance. No one waited to see her credentials and achievements. Joa was not like one of them. She always wore comfortable clothes and footwear. She lived in a soul-conscious state and was happy. Her parents had brought her up like a child and not as a boy or a girl. Only when she entered her teens that it dawned upon her that she was the fairer sex. Well, there are many organisations that are on the lookout for brainy females. She got a job in a reputed firm.

Life was going well for some time. Then, she lost her father in a car accident. Life is unpredictable. Some part of her left with her father. Being the only child, she wanted to perform the last rites. Once again, family and society showed her the mirror that she was the weaker sex. The right to perform the last rites was the domain of the son. Her father will not be able to cross the dimension that helps a soul in uniting with God. She braved the situation well. With her mother's love and unconditional support, she voiced that when her father never brought about this topic, nobody else had the right to bring it up. Her parents were proud of her. Her mother supported her and stood firm by her decision. Joa did the last rites of her father. She realised that her mother, whom she thought was dominated by her husband (her father), had a voice of her own and was a strong-willed lady. One's fragile frame is in no way related to inner strength. Mental strength is far more important, as it's all a mental game.

Moving ahead in the latter half of the third decade, a marriage proposal came from the man, the same boy who had testified in the drug case. She always believed she was not the typical marriage material. However, on her mother's counselling and perusal, she tied the knot. Little did she know there were numerous chapters, more challenging, in her life's book. Once the suffix 'in-law' was added to the woman of the new household, their behaviour changed.

The boy's mother, who seemed to adore her when she had come with the marriage proposal for her son, now viewed her as a threat to her kingdom. The boy's sister who was oozing with love earlier now wanted to make sure that her relationship was with her brother and that the sibling relationship was way superior to Joa's married relationship. Whenever her husband would bring her a gift, her sister-in-law would take it away by voicing loudly that her brother loves his sister more than his wife. Her mother-in-law always stepped in to support this. Her mother-in-law and sister-in-law would behave differently in her husband's presence and absence.

These behavioural changes seemed to upset Joa a lot. On one hand, Joa was trying her best to strengthen her marriage bond with her husband and on the other hand, she was being a victim of gas-lighting. It took her a few years before she realised, this diplomacy was the way of her household. In front of Joa, her in-laws always complained about her husband and vice-versa. This approach was brought to light by her husband when he had differences with his mother.

For the initial few years, Joa was busy raising her children. There was no support from her family. So she created her own support system of helpers. She pushed aside these incidents and involved herself in her profession and children. It seemed she had created an electrified invisible boundary. Throughout her married life, she confided in her mother whenever she felt upset. Her mother always counselled her to focus on the brighter side of life. The larger picture was that her husband loved her and they had two beautiful children. Joa always felt like an outsider.

She would do her professional work and would keep herself busy taking care of the children. Meanwhile, her sister-in-law got married. But she kept visiting their house and tried her best to control both the houses. Her focus was more on her family than her spouse's family. Usually, Joa was not aware of what was happening in her household as her in-laws discussed with her sister-in-law even petty things like the menu to be served if the guests came over. Her sister-in-law was always called whenever guests came for serving and interaction. She was an attention seeker, who would go to all limits to attain this. She even tried to create differences between her brother and their parents.

These things started piling up and Joa felt on the verge of a nervous breakdown. Despite spending more than a decade in this household, it was always about her husband and his sister. She could not see where she fitted in. She wondered whether this was how living with in-laws worked. There was so much hypocrisy, diplomacy, and melodramas. This thought stuck to her and she started distancing herself from them.

Going for long walks or meditating were her ways to release the built-up pressures. Normally, she would retire with a cup of tea on her terrace and introspect. Her favourite lines from a poster in her room flashed in her mind. "God give me the courage to change the things I can! Serenity to accept the things I cannot change and wisdom to know the difference between the two!"

This flashback moment propelled her forward with mightier force than ever. Finally, she could understand the depth of each word. She armed herself with three important tools – courage, serenity and wisdom. From that moment she decided she would not let anyone or anything spoil her mental peace. Nothing was more important than her mental well-being.

She jumped and changed her orbit into a higher realm. From this higher orbit, she felt no emotions for people who had tortured her in various ways all through these years. She felt pity for them as they were spending this beautiful life form as human beings doing petty things. Their motto in life was to eat, drink, sleep, and do loose talk about family members or friends. Their life would be spent doing this. People in slumber behaved like this. It was not her duty to awaken them up. Rather, it was the moment of awakening for her.

She felt a new energy force within her as a heavy burden had lifted off from her soul. She resumed all that she used to love earlier. She sang songs, listened to music and started spending time with herself too. The change was so obvious that nobody could escape sensing it. Her skin started to glow, there was a sprint in her walk and she seemed happy. Her children were overjoyed as they saw a happy, energetic mother as compared to the tired, complaining mother. The romance in her married life was back and she felt very lucky and grateful.

This change brought about a feeling of insecurity in her in-laws' family. They failed to understand this change in her, leave aside appreciating it. They started weaving stories about Joa being in some extra-marital relationship. What else had brought about this change? They tried to feed dirty thoughts in her husband's mind too but he discarded them. Joa realised that a strong-minded, independent woman intimidates everyone and they see her as a threat. All their effort goes into searching for the source of her strength. Such small minds can never realise that strength always comes from within.

Joa realised that the majority of women who live in joint families dealt with such issues, which now seemed petty to her. Although initially, they had seemed so big, that she was almost about to crumble beneath their weight. In our society, one is never taught how to deal with day-to-day challenges. Nobody wants to share their own experiences and ways in which they overcame obstacles. Just as a new bride faces adversities at the hand of her mother-in-law and sister-in-law, knowing fully well that the mother-in-law too was once a newly wedded and that she must have also faced difficult situations. But she chooses not to share and let the new bride go through the same mental trauma. How can we talk about women empowerment when the behaviour of the same woman changes from mother to mother-in-law, sister to sister-in-law, and daughter to daughter-in-law! Is the suffix 'in-law' so powerful that it changes the personality once tagged?

It's time to stop and think. The same woman who loves her daughter despises and shuns the daughter borne by her daughter-in-law. Why are such heinous crimes still happening? The reason is obvious. The majority of women never really try to empower another woman. If one woman has failed to achieve something, there are slim chances that she will share her experiences with another woman for her benefit. A lot has to do with our judgemental society. No one wants to be judged. The root cause is this. If there is a paradigm shift from being judgemental to unconditional acceptance, human relations will improvise. There are very good chances that will lead to bloom time on Mother Earth and there will be unconditional love, care and compassion.

Armed with her three tools—courage, serenity and wisdom—Joa launched a self-help group site by the name, 'Just Me'. This is an interactive session group where women can share their difficult times anonymously and can unburden themselves. Request for discussion with Joa and a counsellor is encouraged so that no woman suffers even in the slightest way as Joa did.

In the case of Joa, the woman who empowered her was her mother and later her daughter. But what about the thousands of women out there with no digital access? To address this issue, volunteers from her group reach out to various rural areas. They empower one woman and encourage her to create more groups and subgroups. Gradually, women start opening up and start sharing their problems.

Joa's efforts are paying rich dividends as her group has started setting various subgroups in different cities of each state. Unconditional listening and acceptance are the keys to making these groups work. Gradually, the message is seeping that till the time women unite, they will always be oppressed and suppressed by their counterpart species. Each woman should hold the baton to educate and empower one woman.

Time is not far when such words like women empowerment will disappear and both men and women will be respected for who they really are. They are the two most beautiful creations of God. The thought behind making them is different, so how can we compare them? Each one is unique.

Joa was living an ordinary life and facing routine adversities. Thinking out of the box led to her transformation. She has helped numerous women so far. She runs a woman-centric organisation where the only qualification one needs is to be a woman who is non-judgemental and is willing to listen and share.

Joa's favourite quotes are:

"Helping others heal is a path to self-healing."

"One should never try to take control of life. Life is meant for sharing."

6

I KNOW YOU ARE THERE FOR ME!

Be God-Loving and Not God-Fearing

There is another dimension of love, which is between a human being and the Almighty. The love we have for our creator. One should be God-loving and not God-fearing. God wants us to have complete faith in him and to love him without any conditions.

Humans have not spared God and always try their best to make an arrangement with him just like some business. This has been a way since times immemorial. In return for the offerings, wishes are placed in front of God. At times, this works in a retrospective manner too, with certain clauses. Depending upon the magnitude of the problem a man faces, offerings are made in a graded manner. A situation like passing an exam has lower offerings than getting a job of choice or even higher for a correct life partner.

Such people have immense faith in the Almighty and are very sure that once they have decided that the offering is equivalent to the difficulty level of their work, God will definitely listen to them. Most of the time, it happens too. I believe it is their faith in God that makes mountains move.

From a distance, this may seem like an act of bribery or like quoting a price for the work. When we come closer, one realises that this game revolves around their unshaken belief in the superpower called God. Just like children lure or bribe their parents, in a similar way humans play the game with the supreme parent, God.

Ever since my perspective changed, the entire picture seemed to have a meaning to it. Now I see these acts of offerings as a man's way of reinforcing himself with faith and positivity. And these reaffirmations get things going. This is pure love in an entirely different dimension where, only one side is existent in real form, whereas the other is formless, invisible. What works is the firm faith of mankind, 'I know you are there for me!'

7

WHO AM I?

Love Without a Story

We have all heard of the saying, "Love thy neighbour." It's time to rephrase it to "Love thy self." Only when we learn to love our own good self can we radiate love for others. Acceptance of oneself is the key. It takes a lot many years before one actually accepts oneself and starts enjoying the journey on this blue planet.

Right from birth, there are comparisons in various forms: be it colour, looks, physique, milestones of a baby, school, college, job, life partner, type of vehicle, clothes accessories, etc. This has no end. The only end one can put is by starting from oneself.

Generally, it's at the twilight of one's life when the question comes to one's mind, "Who am I?" Throughout our lives we live for others, trying to behave and act according to them to please them and fit into the stereotypical society. Regrets towards the fag end of one's life are always full of remorse and guilt.

The right step taken at the right time helps in living a fulfilled life. For this, one needs to introspect and meet oneself daily. One should relate well and be in alignment with the person in the mirror. Only then, we can live the entire circle of life. As the Bhagavad Gita says, we have come alone in this world, and we will leave all this behind alone.

All that we think belongs to us is in reality accumulated over the years. Soon after birth, one tends to utilise the resources available on this planet as Mother Nature accepts us unconditionally as one of her kind. It's never too late to leave behind this competition and start living for oneself.

Only when there will be a shift from outward towards inward, only then there will be love everywhere and this will become a paradise. Let's make a promise to ourselves to love thyself.

8

ARE YOU STILL WAITING?

Love Void!

Few lucky ones experience true love that is above and beyond all human limitations. At times, the love is never expressed but both know their deep love for each other. This dimension of love is pure divine magic.

One retreats in this space and creates one's own world and feels happy. Here the person is the scriptwriter, dialogue writer and director of the whole script. How so ever he wants, in the same direction the story can be steered. Such blissful moments act like boosters when life goes on a slow pace or in some unexplored terrain, which happens often.

This love never actually materialises. It's all in the mind. Those who experience this, feel immense strength and power from this. They feel as if they are in charge of their own lives and feelings. This authority gives them the much-needed lift.

Each one, rather many of us must be harbouring such love for someone. Let's close our eyes, remember that person for a moment and recharge ourselves. The silent question, "Are you still waiting!" always leaves one empowered and happy.

If you have a story, please feel free to contact me. I am still waiting!

9

THE LOVE LESS SPOKEN

Employer-Employee Relation

This is the love between human beings and their house helpers. There are elements of need, love, resentment and anger. This order of elements changes as quickly as the weather. If your helper has been working for a long time, then she is automatically absorbed as a family. There is a mutual feeling of love and care.

This relation is less spoken about as it is always depicted as an employer-employee equation. Each one takes care of the other in silent ways. The employer knows by the walk and body language of her helper of the things going on in her mind, whether she is disturbed or what must have happened the previous night. Depending on her assessment, which a majority of times is correct, she assigns her work.

On the other hand, the helper is also intelligent enough to judge the pulse of the house as soon as she enters. She knows how to impress the lady of the house and what to avoid to keep a positive equation. This keen understanding is nothing less than love as it is mutually of advantage for both of them.

The lady of the house always tries to help in every possible way to uplift the helper worker. Their silent love and understanding always work. It's a mutual benefit relation. Many a time, this acts like a coping mechanism and helps in evolving both.

Let's take a moment to close our eyes and remember that one special person, or maybe more, who has been instrumental in our success.

This love exists, though it is less spoken about. May all of us be blessed with such love in our life.

10

TILL DEATH DOES US APART!

Love Gets a Second Chance

"Till death does us apart" is a vow taken by both bride and bridegroom whenever a marriage is solemnised. The majority of them never realise the true meaning and utter these five words like a talking parrot that repeats. If the bond is between the two souls, then even death becomes just one dimension. True love is rare, especially in a digital world where everything moves at breakneck speed and infinite options are available to everyone. For those who are lucky enough, the Earth becomes truly a paradise.

Such vows were exchanged a decade ago by Sam and Ann. Sam was adopted by his paternal aunt, under tremendous pressure from his paternal grandmother.

His biological mother kept wailing but her screams were unheard in the corridors of their huge mansion. Ann's family had accepted the proposal after knowing all the facts. They enjoyed marital bliss and everything seemed just perfect. They were blessed with two children. Both were doting parents and their family picture seemed complete.

Sam had a biological younger brother who resembled him just like a twin. The relationship between the brothers was estranged as Sam always held his mother guilty for letting him go to his aunt's house and his younger brother Tim always felt distant from him. Everyone's behaviour seemed just right from his or her own perspective.

All of a sudden there was a pandemic and Sam got caught in its sinister clutches. This tragic incident brought his biological family close overnight. His family stood like a rock for him and his wife and children. The effects of the disease progressed rapidly and doctors seemed perplexed. Sam was in intensive care for nearly six weeks. Ann had always had a sheltered life with Sam by her side. She felt lonely and confused.

Unknowingly, Tim found himself attracted to Ann and he offered her a sympathetic shoulder. The trauma of hospital admission was taking a toll on Ann who had left her children with her parents. She would bring them to visit Sam every week or as and when the doctors advised.

There came a time when Sam's recovery seemed promising. Inwardly, Ann felt unhappy when she heard

Sam's progress report. She felt she had betrayed him by developing feelings for Tim. She started finding ways to cut short her visits to Sam and stopped bringing their children to meet their father. It was sheer bad fate that children started looking at Tim as their father figure and never asked for Sam.

Everyone except Sam knew that their lives had changed and now they were three in marriage. Sam's foster parents revealed the ugly truth to Sam, which he could not believe. He called for Ann and his children. After waiting for two days, the attending nurse informed him about the delay in the visit by another week. As if struck by lightning, Sam was able to put all the pieces of his life's puzzle together.

Sam decided to visit his wife and children but was denied permission. Mustering courage, he bribed the night staff boy and went to his home. He was about to ring the doorbell when he heard laughter and excited voices. He hid in a bush, next to the doorway. Suddenly, the main door opened and he saw Ann dressed in the most amazing red evening gown with Tim by her side and the children behind them. They seemed to be going out for dinner. Suddenly Ann stopped and started scanning around her.

When Tim enquired, she said, "I feel the presence of a human being, someone real close." Tim laughed it off by saying, "Don't worry, Sam is in the hospital. I have bribed the nursing attendant to give him medicines in less dosage to delay his recovery." Suddenly the trance was broken by the excited voices of children, "Papa." Sam felt elated and was about to come out of the bushes when he saw his children running towards Tim. This entire evening scene seemed to paralyse Sam. After Ann left with Tim and the children in the car, Sam dialled 911 and collapsed.

What followed for the next couple of days remained a mystery. Sam started showing signs of deterioration. None of the medicines seemed to work and the doctors failed to identify what was wrong. It just seemed that Sam had given up his will to live and was not fighting for his life any longer. Internally, Sam was devastated. The vows they had taken seem to have been forgotten.

His illness was to be blamed or maybe their relationship had a weak foundation. These thoughts kept churning in his mind. All these things led him to the brink of death. Finally, the doctors called for Ann and the children to meet Sam for one last time. Upon Sam's request, doctors told Ann to wear their wedding gown during her visit to the hospital.

Ann seemed perplexed and felt uneasy. Lately, she had a feeling that she was responsible for Sam's condition. On that ill-fated night, she was sure Sam had seen her and their children with Tim. This shock was killing him. As she wore her wedding gown, she was teleported a decade back, to the day of her marriage. She could see Sam, her handsome man, smiling at her. As she came nearer, he extended his hand out to help her climb up the altar. Suddenly, she felt light-headed, and the entire room started spinning. She opened her eyes and found that she was in a hospital emergency room. She had a blackout. And right before fainting, she had screamed Sam's name aloud. Tim had rushed her to the hospital.

She saw her family with sad expressions. She feared the worst. Sam had left his mortal coil on the night she was supposed to visit him in the bridal dress. He had left the last note that read,

"My Ann,

My love was not enough for both of us. With my death, I am setting you apart. Please marry Tim but don't take any vows. Maybe in the next lifetime, we will be together.

Love, Sam!"

11

ONESIE TO WHITE COAT

My Journey as a Doctor

Being born with a womb from a womb is a blessing as well as a curse in our male-dominated world. The struggle to carve a niche for self begins right from the very first breath.

We live in a hypocritical world where one protects one's sister, but for others it's like a wild forest where men roam disguised as wolves. Women abort the girl-child, force others to do it and at the same time look for girls for religious ceremonies. Goddesses hold wealth, education and happiness portfolios. Once you step outside the boundaries of religious places, a woman is eyed as an object of desire. Numerous anecdotes can be written in this context which all girls/women face daily. This is one such story of a brave heart Ira, who lived life on her terms.

Ira was the youngest child in her family. Her complexion and physical features resembled ones living in extremely cold places unlike her parents. She always stood out in family pictures and gatherings. She was compassionate and loved small children. When she was in sixth grade, she decided to become a mother in SOS village where orphans were adopted by willing mothers. Learning this, her parents dissuaded her. She pursued regular schooling and enrolled in a medical school. Besides an excellent academic record, she was unmatched in extra-curricular activities too. The dream of SOS village got buried as she started learning medicine. This was one arena where she could interact with people and help them out. The school was like a fortress and had a protected feel. Once in college, she realised the challenges a girl faces in her day-to-day life. Whistleblowing, snide remarks, lecherous looks, and many times, bad touch.

To avoid prying eyes, she started wearing a big spectacle frame, oiled her hair, braided plaits, and kept an umbrella for her safety. Society is mean and judgemental towards women, the way she dresses, walks, talks, the list is endless. In her college, few of her friends even used to wear vermillion in their hair partition or a *mangalsutra* (an ornament worn by married ladies as a symbol of their marriage) around the neck. The sentiment was that a married girl was less likely to catch a man's eye than an unmarried one. Boys need not make any changes or fear anyone. In their life, such adjustments are not required.

Ira wanted to go abroad for higher studies. Her parents agreed on the condition that she will marry before going. This condition deflated her plans. At the age of twenty-three, she wanted to fly high and explore the world through her own eyes rather than commit. She stayed back in her home country. The twenties is the age when youth is at its peak. Girls get lots of proposals and much more if the complexion happens to be fair. She always thought that she was not a typical marriage material type and refused all. In return, she was cursed and abused for being high-headed and proud.

Not every girl waits for her prince charming. There are many like her who wear their crown and live life on their terms.

Emergency and night duties were scary at times. Trauma patients and alcoholic patients used to never take her seriously and would overlook her. For such patients, only a man in a white coat was a competent doctor. An intelligent, beautiful girl was labelled as incompetent. A person who takes so much time in looking after oneself could not have cracked the exam. Either, it was by fluke or by some unethical means. Ira had to fight against this mindset day in and day out. Even the nursing supervisor gave disapproving looks despite being a woman.

As Ira entered her late twenties, she started enjoying the game of life in the male-dominated world. She knew the rules now and played her cards well. Her father fell ill. To honour his last wish she tied the knot to save her parent's name in society. She silently sacrificed and promised herself to give the best shot in this chapter of her life.

Being a compassionate doctor, she wanted to join the rural hospital in her city. Her in-laws dissuaded her and abused her for making fun of their family. The plea given by her in-laws was, "The house doesn't run on the daughter-in-law's income. They have enough money to provide her food and shelter." These words pierced her heart. She started contemplating the very basis of marriage. She felt like a guest. This was the lowest point in her life. She felt she didn't have a place of her own. Earlier, it was her parents and now it was her in-laws. It struck—the plight of so many women like her who just existed and didn't live life fully.

When the goal is big, sacrifices will be bigger. Ira crushed her dreams and opened a private centre to boost her family's ego. Anything done by choice always gives pleasure rather than when it is being imposed. It was her choice to bow down. She employed women staff who were either divorced or single mothers. Just as the Sun always shines, Ira's name and fame grew and her workplace was acknowledged as the only women-centric place of its kind.

Men patients would often shout or use abusive language at the staff to get the work done for free. Ira's neighbours created all sorts of nuisances to make it difficult for her to work. Acts like blocking her parking space, throwing garbage, or even merely blocking the road in front of her main gate, to deflating the tyre of her vehicle. The boiling point was reached when the workers of adjoining shops would unzip their pants and urinate in front of the main entrance gate. This act was the last straw and she realised it was time to exhibit her power.

Ira had kept quiet all along, following Gandhi's Ahimsa. Now, it was time to show the tigress power. She clicked pictures, uploaded them on social media and complained to the local authorities. This action worked in her favour. It took nearly two decades to get her workplace recognised and respected.

The journey from Onesie to white coat was one hell of a ride but worth every second, and the journey is still on. Ira's love for her white coat helped her overcome all the obstacles in this journey. Love can make mountains move.

12

BUDDY MEET

22 Years, 22 Days and 22 Hours in the Year '22

There are moments in everyone's life when one wishes to grow up once again or beat the age by one or two decades. As one completes more than four decades around the Sun, the vehicle in which one is moving (refer to one's own body) carefree starts demanding one's time and care. Many of us transcend this phase effortlessly and smoothly, while for some it is a bumpy transition. The one factor that helps us immensely is being conscious at the cellular level.

Four of my dear friends lost their parents within a short span of four months. The keen desire to be with them in their difficult times could not be fulfilled due to the pandemic. Three weeks ago, one of my friends called up to share her upcoming visit to her hometown. I casually asked her, "Buddy, what do you want?" Prompt came her reply "You!" I completed our conversation with "Done." I could hear the surprise in her voice, "Oh really!"

The very next day she called to confirm her travel dates. She expressed her wish, "It's been 22 years since we have seen each other, I wish we could recreate those times, even if it is for a few hours only, chit-chat over tea, going shopping and fine dining." I felt like a genie as I replied, "Your wish is my command, my dear friend." And from here upon, all the energy of the universe was diverted to make this happen.

The week flew by, and she arrived. After she had spent the initial few days with her mother, comforting her, and herself, we finalised the date of our magic day. I got my train and flight ticket bookings without any ripples. It seemed as if the universe had conspired and aligned itself to make our magic day happen.

We were supposed to meet at another friend's home. After travelling night and day by all possible modes of transport except by water, we finally met. That moment was like magic. It seemed as if I just opened my hostel room door and my friend stepped in just like TMH days. After a routine exchange of greetings, we prepared tea and sat down on a comfortable couch. How time flew is a million-dollar question. As the Sun started to head westwards, we shook ourselves to the present. Had a hearty laugh about it and went shopping.

It seemed as if we were still living as roommates, just like the residency days. Our silence was also communicative. We headed for fine dining and had a gala time. A mandatory photo shoot was done in between. Finally, when the yawns started creeping in and one of our friend's legs started aching, we realised the moon was planning to give way to the sun.

We hugged each other and felt as if we had lived a lifetime in these 22 hours. Our hearts were brimming with happiness and love. As we were about to head in different directions, my friend exclaimed, "Hey, we are meeting after 22 years and 22 days in the year 2022, for 22 hours."

The other one promptly added, "Now, she (I) will dedicate a write-up to our wonderful meet of Quad 22." Laughing, we headed on different paths, back to where we had come from.

On my journey back home, I felt at least 10 years younger, much happier, contended and rejuvenated. I felt as if I was a new version of my old self or an old version of my new self. Confusing, isn't it? Well, that's the hangover of these 22 hours of intoxication.

My friends know me really well. I dedicate this write-up to my TMH buddies–ASVA (they will figure it out for themselves).

Life is meant to be shared and cherished. Moments spent with friends act like double booster shots. Hope all of you take your shots regularly.

13

SIBLING LOVE!

Twins! Not by Birth

The age difference between my sister and me is never really evident. Although she is two years elder than me, I always feel we were supposed to be born as twins. Somehow, God had other plans and diverged. He sent her alone first and later realised that she needed someone of her own in this journey. So, I was sent exactly two years after her. I am like a shadow to her. Like any other sisters, we support each other unconditionally.

The point is how often do we acknowledge it? Life seems short when one is happy and really long when the ride is rough. In childhood, siblings are inseparable. Teen years demand individual space. College life changes this into a friendly bond. One can share their first crush, first failure, first proposal, awkward moments, in short, all firsts. Your sibling is the first person with whom you can share all your firsts (in a scenario where you have a good relationship). Many a times, the talks are filtered and situations are handled at the sibling level only. One does not need to go to one's parents.

As we walk the path of life, our status changes, marriage happens, and then one's own family and extended family grows. Nearly two decades seem to fly. It is only when one's children start attending college that time seems ripe to rekindle the love again. Although in the years gone by, they have been in regular touch and always provide moral and emotional support to one another. Time lost can never be regained, but yes one can make efforts to keep the bond well connected.

All I can confess now is, that even though we get busy in our lives, there is one part of our heart and brain that always stays glued to our childhood home memories. Thoughts of our parents' and siblings' well-being are always there in the background. As we grow, rather become mature, one tends to express less as compared to yesteryears.

Life is beautiful and love is an emotion that requires expression to keep it fresh and fragrant.

Hope all of us express our love for our siblings, wholeheartedly. Age is just a number. The soul never ages. Stay connected. Express love and let its aroma spread in the garden of your life.

14

TO MY TEACHER, WITH LOVE!

Pure Love for Second Parents

The bond between a teacher and a disciple is divine just like the one between God and his follower. The role of a teacher in a student's life is equally important just like that of parents. One always remembers their first teacher. A teacher can mould a child in many ways. During the schooling years, teachers' words have a greater impact than those of parents.

If a teacher becomes your mentor, then nothing can come in the way and success is guaranteed. If we flip through the pages of history, there has always been a teacher who identified an ordinary child and turned him/her into an extraordinary one. One can read about Guru Vasishtha, Guru Vishwamitra, Guru Dronacharya, Guru Alara Kalama, Guru Chanakya and so on. The list is endless.

Throughout the schooling/training periods, teachers have inculcated strict discipline and mannerisms in their respective students who have made them proud.

The love between a dedicated teacher and student is pure. A good teacher takes pride whenever his students outdo him/her. There is no element of ego. A word of caution here, there are always exceptions. Some teachers are biased and have favourites. This game of favouritism causes multiple issues among the not-so-favourite students, who differ in their thoughts. This write-up aims to evoke positive, motivational vibes only.

I feel I have been blessed with excellent, dedicated teachers during my school and college years. I am connected with a few of my school teachers. Sharing my achievements with them always brings back a school girl's feels.

My college teachers have been my friend and guide, besides being mentors. The level of interaction with them is very much different from what it is with the school teachers.

Here I take this opportunity to be grateful to my school teachers, my medical school and my residency year teachers. I love to wish them every year on Teachers' Day.

Being a learner and a seeker is a very healthy and productive way of living. This philosophy always keeps you active, youthful and energetic.

Take a moment, pause, and think about teachers who have touched your lives.

The next step is to send them a text message or call them. This will do wonders in your body system and the benefits are infinite. The best thing you can gift someone is your time from your busy schedule.

I am sending text messages, what about you?

Let's start with,

"To my dear respected Sir/ Madam,

With love,"

15

IN LOVING MEMORY
OF FLAKE

My Goldfish

Compassion for animals is an inborn trait. My younger child has a soft corner for animals, especially dogs and cats. Living in a nuclear family, as far as I can remember, I was always scared of the boards outside some of the houses—Beware of pets. I still remember that I had stopped visiting my friend's place when she started keeping pets. Such families shift their focus from their guests to their pets. Pets are their family members, just like their own children. And they always defend them.

Since childhood, I am in love with elephants, tigers and chimpanzees. The kinds we can never keep as pets. When I was in primary school, my Popsie asked me about my favourite animals. I mentioned these and requested him to keep them as pets. My father smiled and took me out for a walk in the nearby garden. He asked me to look around. Then he asked my opinion about the idea of a big garden being our house, for our living. I immediately retorted, "Dad, human beings are supposed to live in houses and not in open gardens." He smiled and replied, "If you keep tigers, elephants and chimpanzees as pets, then we will have to stay in the open as the forest is their natural habitat. We can't keep them in our homes. Secondly, there are certain laws pertaining to keeping wild animals. Tiger is an endangered species. We can't keep mighty beasts as pets."

My developing mind could not take it well as to why my father had refused to keep pets. Still, the craze for having a chimpanzee as my buddy was alive in me till my high school days. It's only much later I realised what I had been asking for.

I learnt so many tormenting lessons early in my life, (really? Ha! Ha!), that I decided to honour my children's desire to keep pets. After initial resistance and several rounds of discussions regarding all kinds of possible pets including rabbits, birds, Cheshire cats, etc., we settled for our family's first-ever pet, the goldfish, and then later, an aquarium. It was a welcome change. This little activity kept them busy. They always greeted the fishes early in the morning, before leaving for school and on their return too. Their feeding schedule, changing of the water in the tank, etc., was taken care of by them.

Slowly, the fish started disappearing. It seemed as if the little shark fish was eating them till one fine day all the fish had disappeared. Now we were left with two goldfish in bowls. My son lovingly called one of them Flake. Each living soul has to bid goodbye to this world. My children learnt this lesson early in their lives. The sight of a dead goldfish with bubbles in the water is a disturbing sight to witness early morning. One needs to learn to live with such sights too.

Unknowingly, I had become attached to these goldfish. I always felt I had company and someone was there in my living room. We felt like a family. The day our last goldfish left this world, we mourned. I remarked casually, "This is the primary reason why I don't feel like keeping pets of any kind. One gets attached and, then there is sadness when they die."

My monks replied, "Mom, this is how life is! These pets are teaching us the cycle of life in a very natural way. Try to see from this angle. We get attached, and then we feel sad, but that's fine because we also learn to overcome grief and bounce back in life. Isn't this lesson worth it? It's priceless Maa."

A sense of soothing feeling swept over me. I smiled from within. Children are so pure and naïve that they always see the larger picture and good in everything. I felt immensely blessed and happy.

With full respect, dignity and love, my little monk carried Flake—our goldfish—into our garden. He dug a hole and buried it deep inside. Covered it with mud, offered flowers and suddenly rushed to his room. My heart sank, thinking he must be crying. I decided to wait at the burial spot in the garden itself.

After a few minutes, I saw him walking towards me with a broad smile and a T-shaped wooden stand with something scribbled on it. As he put the wooden stand at one end of the grave, it read,

"In loving memory of Flake!"

Suddenly, it started pouring and we ran inside. I felt God was showering his blessings on my monks.

16

OSCAR'S HOMECOMING!

My Golden Retriever Pup

A baby always brings joy. Be it human or animal. The acts of all babies are surprisingly similar in their infancy and childhood. They are a pure joy to the soul, have a calming effect on the nerves, and create a positive, vibrant atmosphere.

Flake, our goldfish holds a cherished place in our hearts. My little monk kept reminding me that keeping a goldfish was like a teaser and that the real pet was still pending. The thought of keeping a dog always made me uneasy. Pet-keeping discussions during meal times became a routine. My little monk's perseverance and patience finally got him my approval. The main hurdle was overcome. The next important decision was the breed of the dog. This led to discussions with pet owners in my friend circles, online reading and searching for pet stores.

Luckily, we were able to shortlist the breed and gender of the dog. We decided on a male golden retriever puppy. When the time is favourable, one plays the cards well. One phone call connected us with a kennel owner. He had a four-week-old golden retriever pup in search of a home. The deal was done and the day was decided for when the baby would be handed over.

On D Day, everyone seemed to be in a festive mood. It took us nearly half a day to decide the place where our new member would reside. My little monk made the decision easy and clear. His room was cleaned. The puppy's bed was kept in a corner and everyone waited.

As soon as the kennel owner came, everyone jumped with joy. We were advised to maintain silence as the pup was away from his mother for the very first time since birth and was frightened. The carton box was opened. Inside, sat the most beautiful baby I had ever seen (obviously after my monks). Light brown colour with big eyes that seemed scared and doubtful of the new surroundings. Our efforts failed in getting the pup out of the box. The owner suggested we leave the puppy alone in the room and allow him to explore the new surroundings on his own. After an hour or so, he cautiously walked out of the box and sat near my little monk's feet.

There was happiness in our house when my monk screamed, "Maa, Oscar is friends with me now." The naming ceremony was an impromptu one. Oscar liked his name and started responding to it. Everyone else loved our new member. Only I was scared to touch him. He would look with pleading eyes as if yearning for my touch. Oscar knew he had to be in my good books to get his milk and meals on time. He was a naughty pup.

My kitchen area was a forbidden zone, and he knew. It was a lovely sight to watch him walk outside the kitchen, not even once did he cross over. Early morning, he would make a shallow bark and hit on our main door to let him out for his nature's call. My family had a great time with him. He had a habit of lying in my daughter's room close to her feet. Whenever he heard my footsteps, he would close his eyes and fake sleep. This whole act allowed him to sleep in my monk's room. He was always happy in their company.

With my best efforts, I was able to develop a routine with him. We had a strange connection. Whenever I returned from my work, he would jump and come running and just in time stop a few inches away. The scenario was entirely different with my little monks. In four weeks, he grew bigger.

Summer vacations were spent well in his company. Now the time came for school to reopen. The big question was, "How will Oscar live alone in the house for more than half a day?" By nature, the golden retriever breed is family-friendly and loves to be around in the house, pampered and loved.

Finally, I took the difficult decision to find another home for Oscar. Luckily, one of my friends was on the lookout for a pup and Oscar found a new home. Oscar stayed with us for nearly a month and was able to carve a place in our hearts. It's been four years since he found another home. At times, I feel if I had been a little stronger, Oscar would have been with us now. Never knew that even I had a special love for dogs.

After this episode, I realised that love has infinite forms and can be with anyone. It is one of the purest of emotions which requires expression and experience.

At times, we all miss Oscar.

17

THE GREAT PANDEMIC SAVIOUR

The Mobile Phone, My 24 Hours Companion

The last two years have taught us a lot about the unpredictability and fragility of life. With isolations and quarantines, one found solace in one's mobile or laptop and other gadgets. During this pandemic, our love for gadgets resurfaced. The backbone of survival during isolation was the mobile phone in our hands.

Good Internet connectivity was another equally important thing. Armed with these two weapons, numerous human beings have emerged victorious in this battle. For those who could not survive, this gadget helped them in being closer to their loved ones. Barring physical touch, rest everything was real.

The main concern every day was charging one's mobile/laptop and an excellent network speed. A pandemic in the digital era had its pros and cons. The hospital bed status, availability of oxygen, investigations status, etc. were confirmed via this media.

In difficult times when physical human touch was missing, this gadget's touch felt like a family. Their presence and utility revealed their importance. A fully charged mobile phone with high-speed unlimited data has become a necessity rather than a luxury.

It's time to acknowledge and give our *great pandemic saviour*, our mobile, its much deserved due.

18

FROZEN LOVE

Our Love Will Stand the Test of Time!

Time seemed to stand frozen for residents of a small village, Maana. It was at the highest altitude possible, where human life could survive. Due to heavy snowfall for almost six months, the residents had to shift base to areas approximately fifty kilometres downhill. For them, it was a routine year after year. There was a loss of human and animal life. The scenic beauty was divine, which attracted tourists for six months in summer. The main source of income was from tourists. Over the years, residents converted their homes into homestays and rented out rooms or houses for tourists.

A young couple, Shaun and Lea from Athens, Greece, came to celebrate their first anniversary. Lea was seven months pregnant. They had rented a homestay from a local villager, Lhasa, for a month. Shaun, the husband wanted their unborn daughter to be a mountaineer and thought this would be the best way she could connect to Mother Nature. Post dinner, Shaun and Lea were sitting on the patio enjoying hot coffee. Their trance was shattered by impatient calls from Lhasa. He was urging them to go to their rooms as there was a forecast of bad weather with rain and thunderstorms.

Lea got up to go to their room, Shaun requested her to stay for a while, as it was a starry night. They sat with eyes locked in a gaze. Neither of them realised when the sky became overcast and black. They did not see Lhasa coming towards them and shouting to them to move inside, as the wrath of God was inevitable. Suddenly, there was a cloudburst and a gush of water pulled Shaun along. Lea was saved by Lhasa by a fraction of a moment. All their screams were drowned in the thunderstorm. That night was like a scene straight from a Hollywood film.

Lea was shocked and lost her memory. Shaun was untraceable as were other tourists and villagers. Lhasa started taking care of Lea as his daughter. Lea lost her voice due to the shock. After a few days, a beautiful daughter was born. Lhasa named her Shea in memory of Shaun. The most cherished moment of Lea's life passed like a routine moment due to her mental state. She refused to pick Shea or attend to her. Lhasa was left with no choice, other than to bring up Shea. Shea was a gifted child. She was quick to learn about the village lifestyle and adapted well to Lhasa. There were no schools in the village. Lhasa shifted to the plains to give Shea the best possible education. Gradually, his health started deteriorating. He had kept no secrets from Shea. All this while Shea knew Lea was her biological mother and Lhasa was her caretaker.

Just before Lhasa breathed his last breath, he handed over a metallic box to Shea. It contained a few pictures and the boarding passes of her parents. Shea made a resolve to search for her lost identity. The boarding passes bore signs of poor upkeep and had faded in most parts except for the passengers' name, flight number and the date of travel. A lot had changed over two decades in the IT sector and technology. With the help of a friend in the embassy, a search was started to trace the list of tourists washed away in the village of Maana two decades ago. One clue gave led to another and so on. Shea's search brought her to a mental asylum in the city where she found a patient registered under the name of Shaun. Keeping her fingers crossed, she gathered the courage to face this patient.

Her feet felt heavy as she consciously lifted her foot one at a time and inched towards the cell. The guard unlocked the heavy lock and the iron gates opened with a squeaky noise. In front of her eyes, a frail figure was lying on the bed with his back towards the gate. The guard called out, "Hey, Shaun! Somebody has finally come looking for you." Shaun turned very slowly as if this little act consumed a lot of energy. He looked beyond Shea and uttered, "Lea, where are you? I can feel you but cannot see you, Lea, Lea?" And he collapsed on the floor, and Shea caught him just in time before he hit the floor. Her eyes were in disbelief as tears rolled down her eyes. This frail figure was her father who was frozen in time just like her mother.

After completing the formalities, she took her father along with her. With care and medical treatment, Shaun regained health. But his eyes were always searching for Lea. He too had lost his memory due to shock. He remembered only two things, Lea and their unborn daughter. Shea had mixed feelings. The joy of finding her father was diffused because of his inability to recognise her. She considered herself the unlucky child—who was blessed with both living parents, but they had lost their memories.

The idea of reuniting her father with her mother was exciting as well as filled with fears. With the help of doctors, she knew she had to do this part. She planned the meeting to be in Maana village at the same homestay. With the help of her friend, she recreated the same night of horror. This was the best she could do to get her parents out of shock.

With great care and patience, she brought her father. Her friend was already waiting with her mother. Shaun and Lea looked frail with expressionless faces. On the patio, two chairs were kept and an artificial starry night was created. Two mugs of coffee were kept on the side table. With a lot of resistance and hesitation, Shea and her friend guided them towards the chairs. Shaun and Lea sat on their respective chairs.

Spontaneously, they reached out for coffee and their hands brushed against one another.

There seemed to be an electrifying effect in the atmosphere. Both started looking at each other with great curiosity. Suddenly, there was a roaring sound of thunderstorms and rain (as pre-planned by Shea and her friend).

At that very moment, their trance was broken as if the evil spell had been weaned off. Lea was screaming out Shaun's name. Shaun was shouting, "Hold on Lea, hold on." Lea's hand went on her stomach and she started crying uncontrollably. She let out a cry of pain at the agony of losing their child. Shaun bent and kissed her belly, "Baby, we are sorry, we could not save you. It was your dad's idea to come to this place and look what has he done?" Lea lifted Shaun and put her head against his heaving chest. Both were breathing shakily. They sat together, holding hands and crying through the night. Shea was a silent spectator who witnessed her parents mourning her death.

Her friend patted her back and told her to catch up on some sleep. The thunderstorm that had sent her parents into shock twenty years ago had managed to hit them as well as her in some way. The next morning, Shaun and Lea behaved like a newly married couple that had just lost their child, came to Shea and requested the bill for their stay. They were planning to return to Athens after this mishap. Twenty years had vanished from their lives.

They felt some awkwardness in the atmosphere when they enquired about Lhasa. They feared Shea and her friend had done something wrong with Lhasa, as it was Lhasa who had cautioned them regarding the weather forecast the previous night (really! It was way back— twenty years ago). Lea insisted on calling the cops. Suddenly, she froze when she saw her portrait with Lhasa and a small girl. Few other photo frames were there and the little growing-up girl in the frames looked like Shea. Shaun was confused as well.

They walked towards the patio and were taken aback by the sight. Where once mighty mountains stood, were now cramped holiday resorts. There was the sound of machines, making all sorts of noises. On their way back inside, they saw their reflection in the glass.

The young skin had given way to fine lines and wrinkles. Lea looked at her dry cracked skin. She felt her face and ran her hands over her head only to feel thin hair. Once, it boasted of a heavy crop of shiny hair, which had made Shaun fall in love with her.

They walked towards Shea with questioning glances seeking answers to all that had happened in one night.

Shea is still trying to convince her parents that she is their daughter and that they had come out of hibernation after twenty years. With persistence, love, patience and medical help, Shea is hoping for the much-awaited rainbow in her life.

19

BORN TO RULE

Fragrance of Love!

There is a thunderstorm, lightening is playing hide and seek with dark grey clouds loaded with rain waiting for a fierce downpour. The winds are blowing crazily to sweep away the heavy clouds. In the middle of a remote village, a tiny lamp is swaying and trying its best to keep the flame burning. A young lady, Regina is in labour pain, about to deliver. The local village doctor is trying his best to do the procedure in the hut. There is water everywhere and winds are lashing at high speeds. It seems like a near impossible task. "Where there is a will, there is a way" is a famous saying.

Praying to the Almighty, all three of them pledge for a positive outcome. The doctor and her husband,

Richard, help her in pushing. She is nearing exhaustion and almost on the verge of giving up, when her husband gently presses her hand and says, "Dear, just one more effort." The lady closes her eyes and cries out loudly into the wild night. Suddenly, there is the cry of a baby. Finally, the mission has been accomplished and a baby girl takes birth in the small hut on that dark rainy stormy night in a remote village.

The next morning is bright and sunny. Many of the huts have been blown away by the storm, people are stranded, their cattle have gone missing and everywhere, there is a hue and cry. Regina's husband decides to shift to his uncle's house in the city. He packs up whatever little things they have and they set off in their bullock cart towards the city. Near the river, they get down to refill their drinking water.

As Regina alights from the cart, she hears a whispering sound. It seems as though someone is chanting something. She picks up her daughter and goes in the direction from where the sound is coming. Gradually, the chanting becomes louder. She reaches a big tree underneath which a hermit is sitting, chanting religious excerpts from books. As he senses her approaching, the hermit opens his eyes wide and commands her to stop in her path. He gets up from his meditation position and walks towards her. He touches her daughter's feet and starts crying aloud. Regina is confused and in a state of shock. She asks the reason for such behaviour. The hermit calms down and remarks, "All this while, we have been waiting for this pious soul to take birth in human form. She will lead and make this planet a harmonious place to live."

Regina shrugs and replies, "Then why are you crying, oh learnt sage?"

The hermit replies, "Because, I won't be alive till then, to witness the grand moment which will lead to the transformation of mankind and will go down in history as one of the most memorable eras." With this, the hermit leaves and starts walking in the northeast direction.

Richard returns to the cart with water. On finding it empty, he starts screaming aloud and walks towards the forest. There he sees his wife walking towards him with their daughter in her arms. There is radiance around his daughter's head. Their daughter is smiling. Regina shares the prophecy of the hermit and describes her meeting as an exceptional moment. Shrugging his shoulders, Richard takes his daughter and walks towards the cart to continue their onward journey. After two days, they reach his uncle's house. They promise to keep this prophecy a secret.

Years pass by; Richard's hard work and motivation help in getting him a good job. Soon, he starts his workshop. Life is comfortable and the prophecy is deeply buried in their minds. Their daughter, Rachael is a bright and happy child. She is hard working and has a sharp intelligence quotient. Her warm and caring nature makes her win hearts. She always plays with everyone. Her understanding of the body language of birds and animals leaves everyone dumbstruck. The flying birds rest on her shoulder in a carefree way. The pet animals seem to understand her language. Rachel is everyone's favourite.

Once, while returning from school, she witnesses a bad road traffic accident. A lot of people gather but none is willing to help the injured people. She rushes to the site and offers help. After a lot of motivation, few people come forward to help the injured and take them to the hospital for treatment. Her timely intervention leads to the saving of the lives of injured people. After this incident, Rachael withdraws into her shell. Something inside her transforms. She decides to search for the reason for this lack of empathy amongst human beings towards their fellow beings.

Seeing their daughter's change in behaviour, Regina reminds Richard of the prophecy. The more they try to dissuade their daughter, more firm she becomes in her resolve. Finally, she decides to leave the house in search of empathy. Her parents are heartbroken as their only child has renounced the world. However, accepting it as a will of God they promise to support her in every possible way. Somehow, they persuade her to stay with them till she finds her new path.

Rachael goes into a silent retreat and starts meditating. She had learnt from her teachers that "All that you seek outside is within you. God has created a masterpiece by the name of a human being."

After days of meditation, Rachael attains enlightenment. Her aura is so divine that it radiates in all directions. Regina sees an unusually bright light emanating from Rachael's room. She calls her husband Richard. Together, they move quietly towards their daughter's room. The door is wide open. Rachael is sitting cross-legged in a meditative posture and a bright aura is radiating around her head. Suddenly, the hermit's prophecy flashes in Regina's mind. Her daughter had attained the supreme level of spirituality. Rachael opens her eyes and smiles on seeing her parents. Her parents bow their heads in front of her. The image they see now of Rachael is no longer of their daughter but that of a learned hermit.

Rachael sets out on her new path of compassion and empathy. Gradually, her followers increase in numbers. After a few years, she becomes a world-renounced spiritual leader with her centres in almost every nook and corner of the world. Her parent's efforts to give her a normal childhood could not stop her from becoming what was written in her destiny. Her parents move back to their old remote village. Rachael's organisation adopts the village and brings about reforms and changes in terms of building concrete roads, giving good connectivity to the city, constructing a hospital with world-class infrastructure, a school and college, etc.

Every year, Rachael returns to her village on her birthday to be with her parents. Regina can see the hermit's smiling face in the sky giving blessings to her daughter.

20

FERTILISED EGGS

Love for the Future!

I love myself! Adriane thought. She was her favourite and always fantasised about having her replicas. What a beautiful world it will be! With so many fun-loving Adriane's in this universe, what a wonderful place this blue planet will be! With these thoughts in her mind, she rushed out of the shower. Quickly blow-dried her hair, grabbed the first T-shirt and rushed downstairs juggling with her jeans and missed the last step, and boom and thud! She fell flat on the ground. Her younger brother, an ace baseball player, threw a cushion from the living room sofa. Adriane's face safely landed on the cushion and she was saved by a few centimetres.

Their mother came running out of the kitchen and sighed, "Adriane dear, I know yet another idea has come into your mind and you are in an extreme hurry to reach your laboratory. Please try to reach in one piece as an idea without a head is of no use." Her brother giggled. She made a crossed face and went upstairs to change her dress. Inwardly, she was working on her idea of a time capsule and she was just close to finishing it.

After half an hour, she walked downstairs with her head held high and an air of perfection. She sat at the breakfast table. Her favourite fruit juice and scrambled eggs were in front of her on her plate. As soon as her eyes saw the eggs, her face lit up and she knew the day was not very far when she would release her time capsule. She gulped the juice and packed her breakfast. Kissing her mother on the forehead, she picked up her car keys and was on her way to the laboratory. Her cell phone rang. She was so busy in her mind that no other sound was audible to her. As she parked her car in the parking, she picked up her phone to see at least ten missed calls from her professor.

She rushed and went straight to his chamber. Dr Kohler saw her through his monocle, forehead full of creases. He seemed worried. Drumming his fingers on his table, he paused, inhaled and exhaled. After exactly sixty seconds, which seemed like an eternity, he opened his mouth, "So, Dr Adriane, where do we stand right now? We are almost in the last phase of our trial. What do you think we should put in the time capsule? There is immense pressure from the Government, and we are on the verge of running out of funds. We have to release this time capsule within the next eight weeks."

It was Adriane's turn to create a tense atmosphere. She took her time and slowly smiled, "Professor, I know what we need to put in the time capsule."

The professor replies, "Let me hear you out, my dear doctor." Adriane smiled and said, "Dr Kohler, we will put fertilised human eggs from people in different fields. The whole idea is to have the best lot of humans for the future." Dr Kohler removed his monocle and looked up, "Now, what is your criterion for best human eggs?" Adriane replied, "I have a full workup plan for the same. Let's first get assurance from the Government. After that, we will pick up at least five best persons in terms of health, intelligence, looks, etc. from each field of work and call them for assessment. After shortlisting, we will run the data in our software. The computer will do the permutations and combinations. By this, we will have a list of the best eggs and sperms of the human race. The major question that will arise is the consent part. I have created a presentation, which will focus on the benefits of this whole procedure.

Initially, we will keep a hundred fertilised eggs in different stages of development in a one-time capsule. I have another plan. We need to build a bigger time capsule, which can accommodate fifteen to twenty humans from different spheres of work. The smaller time capsule will be created first followed by the larger capsule."

There is pin drop silence as both look at each other. They exchange glances. Adriane's worst fears seem to be coming true. She was afraid that the professor would reject her idea out rightly. Adriane slowly takes her laptop and gets up. As she reaches for the doorknob,

Her professor remarks, "So, Doctor, who are you planning to call upon first?" Tears in her eyes and an expression of disbelief, she cries out loud, "Do you believe in me?"

"Cent percent" comes the reply from Dr Kohler, he continues, "The real challenge is how to convince the Governor and then the people. And, how soon you can start?"

"Sir, we can start immediately, and I promise you that we will do it successfully as long as we work as a team," replies Adriane.

With a sense of accomplishment, she goes to the café. The scrambled eggs have started giving out a fishy odour and find their way in the waste bin. Adriane picks up a cup of black coffee and starts working on her presentation. After working nonstop for many hours, she makes a convincing presentation.

Meanwhile, Dr. Kohler fixes up an appointment with the Governor. Finally, the day comes when their team's hard work of a decade will be presented for the Government's approval.

Keeping fingers crossed, Adriane starts in a motivating manner and manages to capture the attention of everyone throughout. After concluding, the house is made open for questions and answers. There are no questions; everyone seems to be in a state of stupor. Dr Kohler clears his throat loudly to break the silence.

The Governor comes to his senses and remarks, "Dr Kohler, how soon can you start with the selection procedure? This seems to be a noble cause as far as the human race is concerned. Darwin's theory is 'Survival of the fittest', yet another theory says that only the species that adapt to change will survive. Your time capsule will prove both."

He further elaborates, "Please send a quote of how much more funds your laboratory needs. I will get it sanctioned at the earliest."

The gathering disperses. There is a feeling of celebration in the lab.

Dr Kohler invites Adriane the next morning and asks, "So doctor whose eggs will be first on the list?"

Adriane smiles and replies in the affirmative, "Obviously mine, Sir!"

With this, she barges out of the office with a sense of pride in her heart and a smile that finally in her dream project, a part of her, will travel as the first passenger.

21

MY LOVE IS ENOUGH FOR
THE TWO OF US!

Craving for Love in LGBT

High school reunion—these three words cast a magic spell. It's a moment of celebration, which many hearts yearn for, and do preparations for the same. For a few, it's a happy trip down the memory lane. For some, it's an occasion to be completely avoided. There is one class of middle benchers who are happy-go-lucky kind of souls who end up everywhere.

Steve was a healthy boy who was a favourite of his kindergarten teachers. He was good at academics and took part in all extra-curricular activities. He was popular in class. As puberty changes started, he developed a liking for girls and wanted to spend more time with them.

Gradually, he started withdrawing from his boys' group. His keen interest in girl talks and their pubertal changes irked many of his classmates. A complaint was lodged with the class teacher. Steve was left with a strict warning and was ordered to stay with the boys of the class. From a happy, focused child, he became a withdrawn introvert.

To take things under control, his parents changed his school. But his heart was in his old school. He took admission again in the next session. This time he seemed confident and happy. He had long hair, just like pop stars, and always smiled. Pubertal changes were missing in him, which normally happen in boys of his age. He had silky smooth facial skin and there was no sign of any beard or moustache. Everyone labelled him as a case of delayed puberty and never bothered him. The high school period came to an end. Everyone exchanged their slam books and left with a promise to be in touch for the rest of their lives.

Fast forward ten years. In some places in the western world, a glamorous top model walks down the fashion show ramp with utmost grace and poise. The crowd is cheering madly and calling her name "Stevie". Suddenly, the journalist (Alan) in the first row who is there to cover the fashion show wakes up from his trance. This name sounds familiar. He scratches his head and fails to remember and pinpoint the connection. The next model walks down the ramp and so on and the show goes on. At the post-show dinner, he meets with Stevie and is swept off by her beauty. There is a sense of faint familiarity. Thinking it to be the after effect of alcohol, the journalist goes home. Before going home, he exchanges his mobile number with Stevie.

The next morning, Alan wakes up with a severe headache and is unable to get Stevie out of his mind. He prepares black coffee and sits at his working desk. Scrolling through the Internet, he is unable to procure information beyond ten years. This sets him thinking, that there was some mysterious past of Stevie. The more he tries to kick Stevie out of his mind; the thought comes back like a boomerang. He makes up his mind to dig out the past. He starts dating Stevie over coffee and movies. Somehow, Alan is unable to go beyond the dry good night. He is more determined and decides to check her apartment in her absence.

On a routine coffee visit to her house, he manages to get her house keys' impression and gets a duplicate key made. Once she is away on a weekend shoot to a distant place, Alan stealthily enters her house and begins his search. There is no record of her childhood/school days. As he was about to abandon his search, an old album drops from the top shelf. Immediately, he recognises it to be his school album. He glances through the school class pictures. He is spellbound by what he sees. This was his class picture. He could recognise himself, but there was no face like Stevie. Alan takes out his magnifying glass and scans all the children's faces. He finds a striking resemblance with Steve. A chain of thoughts clouds his mind— "Is she Steve's twin sister or is she Steve himself?"

He stumbles, gets up, and leaves the house. A notification icon on his mobile breaks his trance. There is a mail from the high school alumni group informing us about the high school reunion in a week. Alan is perplexed by the recent discovery. He texts Stevie requesting her to be his date for the reunion. There is no reply. He impatiently waits for Stevie's return.

Unable to hold the suspense any longer, Alan goes to the airport arrival lounge to pick up Stevie. She seems visibly impressed by his gesture and smiles. They drive to a nearby restaurant for lunch. Alan pops up the question about his high school reunion. She stops eating in the middle and excuses herself to go to the restroom. She goes to her house. Alan patiently waits for half an hour at the lunch table. He requests the lady staff to check the ladies restroom. To his dismay, there is no one in the restroom. For the next few days, he is unable to contact Stevie as she had blocked his mobile number.

His fears seem to be coming true. He gathers all his courage and goes to see her at her house. After much perusal, she opens the main door. The sight Alan sees is heart rendering. Stevie is standing in front of him with swollen eyes, her eye makeup had smudged all over her cheek, her hair was unkempt and she was sobbing. Seeing her in this state, Alan's heart sank and he hugged her tightly in his embrace. Slowly she looks up and remarks,

"Alan, I had a crush on you since kindergarten. Do you remember Steve? The boy who enjoyed the company of girls, changed school, returned and became an introvert!"

Alan was silently listening, waiting for her to continue and complete. She continued, "Alan I am Steve! Do you still love me?" The ground below Alan's feet seemed to give way and he lost his balance. His eyes popped out in disbelief, "Stevie, you are the same old Steve, now a top model! Oh gosh! I fear this."

There was silence for a few minutes, which seemed like an eternity. Finally, Alan spoke, "So, that's the reason you were avoiding the high school reunion? Now I understand your inhibition. Well, I respect this and promise that we will never let the past spoil our present. Will you be my date Stevie for the high school reunion?"

Stevie smiles shyly and gives an affirmative answer. Post dinner, she reveals the difficulties she faced due to her inclination towards being a female. So, she left her hometown and settled in a distant place. Got the required surgery done and gave herself a new identity. Both of them locked their hands and looked up to God. High school reunion here we come, Alan with his date Stevie.

The true identity of Steve was never disclosed, and everyone enjoyed the reunion. Alan was eager to show off his most beautiful date. Stevie never wanted to be recognised as Steve and enjoyed the party as his date. Alan's love was true and enough as they accepted each other unconditionally.

22

AN EMOTIONAL RISING

The Call of Love

Just like tsunami slashes and disrupts whatsoever, who sever comes its way; similarly, an insight into our past causes a blast in our present.

A dynamic, enthusiastic, young girl in her mid-thirties is a new entrepreneur holding a high position in a multinational company. With her head held high, looking up at the sky, she seems to glide on the ground. Lady luck is shining bright on her side. After all, she worked really hard with grit and determination to be in the position she is in. Despite limited resources, she climbed up the ladder of success, much to the astonishment of her colleagues.

Soon, she was the new vice-president of the leading law firm.

One day she received a letter from an unknown source dated twenty years ago. Moments of suspense followed as she slowly opened the seal. There was a birth certificate from a government hospital in a distant town. Her hands trembled as she slid out the certificate with a covering letter. She recognised her mother's handwriting instantaneously. Her mother had addressed the letter to her.

The letter read as,

Dear daughter,

If you are reading this letter, it means I have left for my heavenly abode. I pray to God that you must have achieved whatever you always wanted to achieve and must be riding the success wave. (Tears started rolling down her cheeks. She knelt and started crying loudly. This Christmas, she had made plans to reunite with her mother and reconcile. Now, this letter was like a tight slap on her face. Restoring her courage, she continued reading).

Sarah, my daughter! Do you remember, I used to buy toys in twin sets? And you used to ask me the reason. Well, darling, the truth is, I gave birth to twins. Yes, Sarah! You have a brother who also happens to be your twin. God had other plans for him. Sam, your twin brother was born with Down Syndrome and needed special care. Your father was not willing to keep him and we had continuous fights over this issue.

One fine day, when I was nursing you, my mere six months old angel, your father snatched you from my arms and stormed out of the house. I did not see him after that. Some common friends used to give me news about you. I was left all alone with Sam.

Life had hit a rough patch and unwillingly, I had to put Sam in an orphanage for children with special needs. I came to know that you always despised your mother for she left you when you were six months old. Sarah, my love, please remember your mother always thought about you every living second. I thought of explaining all this twenty years ago when you were in high school.

Do you remember my love? Your father once again intervened and you left without looking back. I had given this letter to your father. I know the letter never reached you, as you never contacted me.

I wrote another letter and kept it safe with my lawyer with instructions that it should reach you when I am no more. So, you see, I never did any wrong to you or your brother. The situation was difficult and this was the best I could do as a teenage mother. My lawyer will get in touch with you to hand over my house (my sole possession) and my car keys to you.

You will see a twin almirah in my room named Sarah and Sam. All the gifts for the last thirty years are there for both of you. This birth certificate will stand by my truth. You can ask your father too. He will explain the whole truth. Please forgive your mother and your brother Sam.

I am writing down the address of the orphanage where Sam lives. Now he is the general manager of that orphanage.

If you can forgive me in this lifetime, my darling, please arrange a prayer meeting in the church after my funeral, so that I may rest in peace. Please bring Sam along, and your father too if he willingly drops his anger towards me.

Please remember, Mom always loves you, remembers you and is always proud of you every single moment.

Love,

Mrs Smith

(Your mother)

By now Sarah was inconsolable. She had always thought that her mother her left her for greener pastures. This story was told by her father since childhood and endorsed by her paternal grandparents. When her father was fighting for his life last year when he was diagnosed with a brain tumour, he was often seen mumbling, "I am paying for my sins! God, please forgive me." He had stopped recognising her and used to call her Sam. Gradually, he lost his speech coherence. Her last memory was of her father's fingers pointing towards the sky and seeking forgiveness with folded hands. Thereafter his soul left his body.

This letter was like an electric jolt for Sarah. All these years she had hated her mother for leaving her as an infant. Now the truth was clear in front of her eyes. She could visualise the entire life her mother might have had to face, being a single parent and later being single. She wiped her tears and read the birth certificate. A feeling of bliss and happiness ran from her head to toe. At this very moment, she forgave her mother and father. Both had their reasons and behavioural responses.

She placed the letter and the certificate inside the envelope carefully. She cancelled her meeting schedule for the whole next week and booked a flight to the city where the orphanage was. As soon as her aircraft landed, her heart started pounding at the mere thought of meeting her brother. This feeling of "I am not all alone", gave her immense power. The airport taxi was waiting at the pickup counter. She settled and let the wheels of the car take charge. City roads gave way to countryside roads, lush green trees and bushes swayed with gentle wind as if playing. Sunrays played hide and seek. Slowly, the taxi manoeuvred through the curvaceous path, and she found herself right in front of the orphanage.

Gathering courage, she asked for the way to the general manager's room. The bell boy smiled and said, "We all knew you will come one day. Sorry to know about Mrs Smith's demise."

Sarah was taken aback. As she entered the room, the chair rotated, and she felt as if she was in front of the mirror. Sam was an identical twin. Sam gave a confused expression. He exclaimed, "Sarah, my little sister, not so little now."

Sarah felt an ocean of emotions and heaviness in her heart as if her chest would explode. She regained her calm pose and hugged her brother. She felt complete. What life was not able to do, death had done.

Bidding farewell to the orphanage, she flew back with Sam. They rested their mother's coffin near their father's grave with the message, "Life kept them apart, united by death: Mr & Mrs Smith." The prayer meeting was attended by family and friends. Sarah felt her mother smiling from the abode of the Lord.

Sam went back to the orphanage and she continued with her work in the city. Both looked forward to celebrating Christmas at their mother's house. The mere act of opening one letter from the past, changed Sarah's attitude towards life forever.

She realised that the thought that she had a sibling gave her immense power and strength. Blood relations are deeply connected as they are created by divine intervention. This love is in another realm as the origin is from the womb.

23

MY FIRST LOVE

Love for Travel

The trance of a hot summer evening was broken by the cries of a new born. Many years ago, somewhere in a government hospital in the maternity ward, a lady gave birth to a beautiful child, fair as ice and with a smile like the Buddha. The day she was born, her mother had noticed a wheel-like configuration on her right sole. She had remarked, "My daughter is born to travel far and wide, travel will be her first love." This little girl was named Trivia.

She was a beautiful, cheerful happy child. During her early childhood years, she would spend time exploring every nook and corner of her house and the play area. The sight of birds, animals and plants stimulated her, and she always yearned to go out of the house. She excelled in school—in academics as well as in extra-curricular activities. Her favourite hobby was organising school picnics and trips. Her parent's life mantra was to travel to different places. Exploring new places, meeting new people and witnessing different cultures were the most invaluable lessons in any child's life.

Trivia had a habit of writing all details of her travel in her personal diary. By the time she became a major, her diary was beaming with many itineraries. She was all set to explore the world on her own. She joined a reputed flying school and became the ever first lady pilot from her state. Her passion for travel earned her high-flying mileage scores in a short duration of time. This led to the shifting of her department from flying to the non-flying area, ground staff.

Her heart beckoned her. She took early retirement and set up her travel consultancy by the name of Trivia Travels. She is busy helping people realise their love for travel.

24

LOVE- A GAME OF CHESS!

Love Beyond Boundaries

A slender silhouette is seen standing on the Howrah Bridge, seeking conversation with the roaring Hooghly River. There is no one in sight, except for a security guard on one end of the bridge. There is complete darkness. The only saviour is the moon admiring itself in the calming waters of the Hooghly River. All of a sudden, the spell is broken by a loud thudding splash. The security guard turns his head towards the sound and all he can see is a figure falling into the giant river. It seemed as if a child was going in the arms of her mother. The river had invitingly opened her arms to catch her child falling off the bridge. It seemed as if, Mother River wanted to save her falling child from the ills of the world.

The alarm goes off. Shashwat yawns and stretches his arms outwards and hits the snooze button. This dream was recurring every night. He racked his brains to get to the root cause of this dream. He kept lying on his bed looking at the ceiling fan. The fan seemed to make a squeaking noise as if trying to replay the part of Shashwat's life that was missing.

The trance is broken by some hushed whispers from the street. Shashwat slowly parted the curtains of the window. What he saw made him jump out of his bed. A young girl's body was lying across the road. Many people had gathered around her. She was wearing a white cotton dress with blood on her body. The girl raised her hand with great difficulty and pointed towards Shashwat's window before she collapsed into oblivion. Everyone started staring at his window. This sight confused him. He was a new entrant in this neighbourhood and hardly recognised anybody. Police were called and statements were taken from onlookers. The girl's body was sent to the forensic laboratory.

Suddenly, there was a firm meaningful knock on his door. Shashwat quickly changed. As he was buttoning up his shirt, the door flung open. Two police officials flashed a search warrant on his face and started searching his house. His pleads of not guilty fell on deaf ears. Police recovered a marriage photo album. To his surprise, the bride was the girl who had just died on the street. The bridegroom's face was hidden in all the available pictures. With this evidence, he was taken into police custody for interrogation. He pleaded for his innocence. There was no evidence to support this. Apparently, on the interrogation of the witnesses, none seemed to recognise the girl. It seemed like an open and shut case of a newly married couple where the husband had murdered his wife or there was an abetment to suicide. Shashwat was imprisoned for life.

A quiet morning with an earlier bad dream seemed to have happened or was it still a dream? He pinched himself so hard that he screamed out loud. A newcomer in the city of Kolkata with no alibi or any contact, it seemed Shashwat had caught himself in quicksand with no ray of hope. Days went by and he could not find a way to prove himself not guilty. After about a month, another prisoner was moved into his cell. This man had long unkempt hair with a long beard and moustache. His face was barely seen. Shashwat was sceptical about his new jail mate.

After a few hours, the prisoner makes the first move and comments, "You are Shashwat, right! The man who got imprisoned for no crime." And he turned his back towards Shashwat and faked as if he was sleeping. Shashwat was dumbstruck. He could not believe his ears. He went towards his inmate and gently touched his hand, "Who are you?" There was a mischievous laugh followed by a dry cough. The inmate smirked, "I am your saviour. God has sent me to prove your innocence." Shashwat fell on his knees and started crying bitterly.

The prisoner replied, "I am Bijoy, brother of the girl who had committed suicide. And I know you are innocent. So, I have come here on a false pretext of a robbery to save you." Shashwat replied in disbelief, "But why? Why is there a sudden change of heart? Who is making you do all this?" Bijoy took a deep breath and gestured to Shashwat to sit down. He sighed and continued, "It's a long story and after listening to this you will get all your answers, including the one related to your recurring dream."

Shashwat started feeling nervous and an uncomfortable feeling swept over his entire body. He did not remember any of his past. All his memories were recent, only of those of his life in Kolkata. The moon started to peep through the high round window and a tree twig could be seen and heard gently tapping on the windowpane. There was a stony silence. It seemed like an eternity before Bijoy finally spoke up.

There was a village around hundred miles from Kolkata. A rich merchant had two sons. The merchant's loyal house servant had a daughter and two sons. Bijoy was one of them. Shashwat was the younger son of the merchant. Everything was going on fine for quite many years. The time came for Shashwat's elder brother, Shiva to leave the village and go to college. Shashwat was still in high school. Both brothers had a striking resemblance. People used to mistake one for the other. In college, Shiva got infatuated with a girl named Moushami. Both of them were unaware of the fact that she was the daughter of their household servant. Things went on fine for a few years. Finally, college life ended and Shiva went abroad for higher studies. For him, it was more than a usual college affair. Little did he know that even Moushami was serious and had silently dedicated her whole life in his name.

A few years went by but there was no communication from Shiva. Meanwhile, Moushami kept waiting and refused all the marriage proposals that her parents came up with. One day, she was crying along the bank of the river when Bijoy spotted her. On asking the reason for her behaviour, Moushami started weeping inconsolably and narrated her entire love story. Bijoy persuaded her to forget Shiva as he was rich and they were their servant's children. Moushami revealed she had conceived Shiva's child before he went abroad. Shiva was unaware. Even she was not aware till her third month. By then, it was too late to go for termination. So, she had no choice, but to continue the pregnancy. She had given birth to a baby boy, whom she named Shivam. Due to her unmarried, single status, she had to give up her son to an orphanage.

Life was weighing hard on her. On one hand, there was pressure from her parents for marriage, on the other hand, she was desperately waiting for news from Shiva. A common college friend told her about seeing Shiva in Kolkata. She left for Kolkata and reached the address given to her. She rang the bell. Her heart was thudding hard against her chest. She had waited so long for this moment.

Suddenly, the door opened and she was greeted by a maidservant. A voice echoed in the hallway, "Who is it, Lakshmi?" This voice sounded familiar to Moushami. She pushed the maidservant out of her way and walked with hurried steps inside. The person she saw looked like Shiva but his eyes failed to recognise her. Moushami tried to hug him but was politely pushed aside by the man. He gently asked, "Ma'am, do we know each other?"

This statement seemed to hit Moushami like lightning and she started crying. In between her cries, she narrated the entire story of their love in college and the birth of their son. Before the man could explain anything, she rushed outside. Shashwat realised that Moushami had mistaken him for Shiva. He started running after her. God seemed to have taken an offence and it started pouring heavily. Moushami rushed towards Howrah Bridge and climbed up on the railing to jump. Shashwat tried his best to explain it to her but his voice was drowned in the downpour. In the flash of a moment, he saw her jumping off the bridge. Suddenly, there was a blackout. His last memory was that of a girl in a white dress, jumping off the bridge.

Bijoy paused and stared at Shashwat. "Do you remember anything?" he asked Shashwat, who looked blank. Shashwat could not relate to any of the characters or incidences. All he could remember was that he lived in the neighbourhood and had no contacts. He seemed to have amnesia after some head injury. Bijoy started getting impatient and tried to convince Shashwat about the whole story, without any success. He further added that he was following his sister and had himself mistaken Shashwat for Shiva. Bijoy had hit him with a hard rod as revenge for his sister. Only when Shashwat had fallen on the rainy ground, did Bijoy realise his mistake. But it was too late by then, as the security officer at the other end of the bridge had already raised an alarm. Suddenly, there were dazzling bright lights of torches, with the sound of approaching footsteps. Bijoy had to run to save his life.

The next day newspapers headlines flashed a young woman being saved by a group of fishermen on the rainy night. By this time, Bijoy had eloped from Kolkata and went into hibernation. Moushami was taken to a government hospital. Little did she know, Shashwat was also admitted to the men's ward in the same hospital. Due to trauma on his head, all his memory had been wiped off. He was diagnosed with total amnesia. There was no past, only present. By fate of God, destiny again brought both of them together at the time of discharge. Moushami could not bear the blank look in Shashwat's eyes. She was unaware of the fact that she was mistaking Shashwat for Shiva.

As a last attempt to convince Shiva, she confronted him. She narrated their college life love to the birth of Shivam. She proposed marriage and talked about bringing home Shivam, their son from the orphanage. Shashwat gently told her that he did not recognise her. At that moment, Moushami pledged she would seek revenge. She felt betrayed in love and the only solace she could find was in revenge.

She followed him to his house. Police had traced her through her identity cards. She rented a house across the street from where she could see Shashwat's bedroom window. She patiently tried all possible ways to catch his attention. All attempts went in vain. All this while, Shashwat started getting dreams, which troubled him a lot. After about a month or so, Moushami committed suicide by consuming poison and laid her life in front of his window with her hand pointing directly towards Shashwat's window, thereby directly blaming him for her death. This was her grand revenge for the great betrayal.

When Bijoy came to know of this, he realised Shashwat was innocent. To absolve himself of his guilt, he planned his arrest and got himself in the same cell as Shashwat. Bijoy gave a statement in favour of Shashwat, which led to his release from prison. Shashwat felt relieved as well as confused about the whole story. Nothing seemed familiar. He searched for Shivam and after legal formalities, adopted him. This was his way of paying respect to the departed soul of Moushami. Things went on well for quite some time and Shashwat became a single parent handling his career and house efficiently.

Life is unpredictable. Shiva returned from abroad and went straight to his native place looking for Moushami. He was in a great hurry to meet Moushami, the love of his life. He wanted to ask her the reason for not replying to his letters and calls. His suitcase and flowers dropped from his hands as he entered Moushami's house and saw her photo in a frame with a flower garland. His head started spinning and he almost fell. He was caught by Bijoy in mid-air, just before he hit the ground.

Their eyes were filled with questions. Bijoy narrated the entire story and the incidents leading to Moushami giving up her life. The question that puzzled both of them was, why Moushami never received his letters or calls. Both were unable to understand. They saw a frail old man's figure with a stick in hand, walking towards them. On seeing Shiva, the old man broke into tears and begged for forgiveness. Being a servant in their household, he had assumed, Shiva was using his daughter Moushami for pleasure and would leave her once he found a girl from an affluent family. The old man was blinded by his humiliation at the hand of Shiva's father. So he had created a wall between his daughter and Shiva. He never showed Shiva's letters to Moushami nor did he convey his calls. In a fit of rage, to take revenge from his master, he ended up losing his daughter. The old man never realised that his revenge had affected more than four lives—Shiva, Shashwat, Moushami, Bijoy and even little Shivam, besides his own life.

Later in the evening, Bijoy and Shiva went to Kolkata to meet Shashwat and his son Shivam. Shashwat recognised Bijoy as his prison cellmate but failed to recognise his own brother Shiva. Greetings exchanged, Shiva hugged and blessed Shivam. He could see that Shivam was a perfect blend of Moushami and him.

With a heart full of memories of his beloved Moushami and his son Shivam, Shiva left Shashwat's place and decided to go abroad and never come back. Right before leaving, he made Shivam his heir and Shashwat the caretaker of his property in India. Bijoy helped Shiva in all legal formalities.

With all the legal property papers in his hand, Shashwat gave a demon-like laugh. After all his hard work of so many years, his patience had finally borne sweet fruit. His little secret of being in love with Moushami and being the father of Shivam was safe and secure in his heart. All through his childhood and teenage years, he was compared with his elder brother Shiva, who was the apple of their father's eyes. This comparison suffocated him and all this while he was planning revenge. Bijoy's father unknowingly helped him in his mission. No one ever came to know that Shashwat had robbed Moushami of her modesty many times on the pretext of helping her meet his brother. He was the reason behind her suicide.

As Shashwat stood on the Howrah Bridge, with his son in his arms to pay obeisance, River Hooghly soared high with all its might as if to express her anger over the numerous betrayals she had been a silent witness to. Man's blind love, ego and lust led to the weaving of such a complex plot, which led to betrayals and acts of revenge, leaving many lives sad, incomplete and unfulfilled.

25

INKED WITH SOUL

Straight from a Loving Heart

My love,

We made a promise to each other many years ago. Unlike others, we committed to 'rise in love' and not fall in love. Is love sufficient to hold us together? Do you feel we have become distanced from our vow? These days I feel we are not in the same space. We are physically together, yet not in the same mental dimension. The things which we enjoyed doing together seem like a distant lifetime. Is this a part of growing together or has the pandemic drifted us apart? At times, I feel do you really remember the first time we met?

When I first saw you, I felt a peculiar sensation, which I never experienced before. During my college days, many boys approached me. But I always felt that I did not need a man to complete me. So, I politely refused all the offers that came my way. When I saw you, I experienced some deep feelings and I wanted to touch you. Such kind of emotion was unknown to me. I committed myself to you at that very moment. You were the first person whom I allowed to touch my hand.

Ours looked like a fairy tale story in the beginning. Now I think, we always talk about a perfect match, perfect romance and the popular last line of such stories—They lived happily ever after. Reality is far different from fiction. Initially, we were awestruck and considered ourselves a lucky and handsome couple. Honeymoon days usually give way to reality checks. I have often heard that for a man, marriage is like the phase of being settled, it's the end of the race to find a suitable life partner. He no longer feels the need to express and shower his affection frequently. For a woman, marriage is the beginning of everything in her life. The expectations are very different. The mindset of both is poles apart. Differences are bound to creep in if both or at least one of them is not alert.

Deep inside, I know that you love me a lot and take pride in how I am raising our children, and looking after the family, besides my professional commitments. I know you are committed to me and make all efforts so that we have a comfortable living. Once in a while, I need to hear words of appreciation from you. After my parents, you are the one person whose opinion matters to me the most. I need your approval on many of my things. I want you to be involved in our children's lives as much as I am involved. After all, their childhood will not come again. It happens only once. I am not trying to change you or find faults in you. You are perfect in every way and I love the way you are. But yes, I need you to comfort me at times when I have had a bad day or just sit beside me holding my hand and say nothing. There is still a part of me that I feel you have not touched. Is it that we are losing the spark in our relationship or it's just forties blues? I wish you could understand that a simple smile or nod when I serve you tea or meals is enough to energise me. These simple acts work like a dash charger and I get supercharged.

I understand you are busy with your professional work and your stock market investments. I hope to fit in somewhere. Now the time has come when I need to ask you, "Are you in a mood to talk?" before I can speak my heart out. If I sit with you, it means, I want to spend quality time with you. During that moment, a simple act of keeping aside your television remote or mobile makes me feel that you still cherish my company.

During the last two decades, we have been busy raising our children and I feel we have lost touch with each other. Normally, I manage my affairs very well and you know that. Yet, if I call you during working hours, it means I have something really important to talk about. If you call back, it reflects I am important to you. Please don't get me wrong that I am complaining. I have observed the way you talk to your friends or your office people. You are always polite and patient. But, whenever you talk to me, I sense urgency or hurry in your voice. At times, I feel I don't know you I am an outsider. There is a part of you, which is not known to me. We work towards the same goal of well-being of our family.

You know I am a morning person and in my best state in the morning. You are an evening person. Our levels of energetic states don't match. But this is what happens with most married couples. Opposite poles attract, isn't it? I feel our minds have been programmed by this theory since childhood. What's the harm in having similar choices or doing similar activities? It's so much more fun. You enjoy each other's company more. We never go for walks together. Our walking speed doesn't match. We have the same goal to reach home together. Can't you reduce your speed to match my speed? You are taller than me and your stride length is bigger compared to mine.

These little things have never bothered me earlier, maybe because I was too busy with our children. Now since the children are teenagers, I feel a void. I have tried to share this with you so many times. But you have always dismissed me by saying that I overthink a lot and need to relax. I introspect and work on improving myself. In this endeavour, I have done a few self-improvement courses, besides doing meditation regularly. I need you to say to me often, that you love me.

The forties are a difficult phase of life, a period of transition. During these years, where on one hand our children, who are in the growing up phase, need us a lot more, on the other hand, our parents start to age and need our attention too. Somewhere in between, we tend to lose ourselves. This should be identified and rectified at the earliest.

There is a very famous proverb, "A stitch in time, saves nine!" Now, I realise its depth and real meaning. Marriage is like an institution; it's a lifelong commitment of two souls who decide to spend their lives together. I feel each one of us needs a witness to this fantastic phenomenon called life. So, we come together and get married. This should age like wine. There is no secret recipe for a happy, successful marriage.

Each marriage works on its own dynamics, which only the couple decides. The rules and terms vary from couple to couple. So, the best is never to imitate other couples. By this, I want to share that I don't like being compared with another's spouse. One needs to accept each other as they are and not try to change the other person. To understand someone's behaviour one needs to see their childhood life and the environment in which that person has grown up. This little act of empathy works wonders in understanding the other person.

If there is something you want to convey in an unpleasant tone, please convey it when we are alone. It's humiliating to be shouted at in front of your children or your workers and helpers. Being adults, we both know deep in our hearts that we are not doing something wrong or unethical. We can always sit together and sort out the differences. If I don't agree with you on any point, it doesn't mean that I am trying to oppose you or argue. My point of view will be different many times. We must respect this difference. After all, we must learn to agree to disagree. There are times when you override the commands, which I give to our house staff. Please remember that I keep quiet to maintain marital harmony. It doesn't go down well.

I left everything, my essence, to be with you and ignored my relations from my parent's side for so many years. In all these years, I managed to accept your relations and bonded with them. But, I don't see you bonding in return. It hurts when my parents are not respected well or you feel annoyed whenever I visit them. For once, please think about how you will feel if you didn't meet your parents or your siblings for months together. I have a heart that beats for my parents and my siblings besides our children and you. It will be very thoughtful of you if you can let me visit my parents whenever I wish to. I need not take permission from you nor do I need to give you an explanation of why I want to meet them. Simply, my wish to meet them should be enough.

Before marriage, I always celebrated all my festivals at my home. I am used to the style of my house. Just because I am trying to understand your family's ways, doesn't mean I don't know things. Each household is different and so are their ways. My efforts to adopt your house practices will take time. At times, I just cannot adopt certain things, which I don't find practical or liberal. Helping me will be beneficial rather than criticising me. If your sisters know the ways of your house, it's obvious. Please refrain from comparing me with them.

Our childhood and upbringing were tangentially different. Let's learn to accept the beauty of our differences. This makes us unique. You know, my day revolves around you and our children. You should feel blessed that your spouse is sincere and committed. What more do you want? Please explain to me in a low voice. One needs to raise his voice only if he feels distant (in a mental state). Otherwise, a soft voice is heard far better than a harsh, loud voice.

I am at a point in my life where I don't like what I see in the mirror. I have scars from childbirths, fine lines on my face and a little bit of increase in midriff girth. Earlier clothes don't fit well. The youth is showing signs of a life lived well and fully. These are physical features that my soul doesn't recognise. In my memory, I am still that college girl with glowing, healthy, supple, skin and a slender, toned silhouette. I never realised when this new person started looking at me from inside the mirror. The brain recognises and the heart refuses to believe. This is a transition phase in my life. I want to overcome this with you by my side. I need reassurance that you still love me for who I am in that moment. Is it asking too much?

Once in a while, we can go for walks or go for a coffee date. Beauty lies in the eyes of the beholder. Many times, I look at myself through your eyes. Have I become a necessity in your life? We should sit together and talk about our insecurities to rekindle the spark, which has gone dim or may be missing.

I will wind up by conveying that the promise we made with each other when we met, it's time to reinforce it back in our lives. I know we love each other a lot and are preoccupied at times. So, the best option seems like being quiet to have less interaction to avoid the unnecessary eruption of any volcanoes. The molten lava that erupts destroys our mental peace for the next few days. The best is to remind oneself and convey, "I am having one of those challenging times, this too shall pass." This will be like an alarm signal.

Let's pledge to 'rise in love!'

Forever yours,

Lovingly,

J.

26

TOUCHED BY LOVE!

Not a Summer Fling!

Summer times evoke lots of varied emotions and memories. For some, it is calling to the mountains, for some others the beach and it's just hitting the pools in their homes/areas for yet others. Summers echo with words like water, fresh lemonades, chilled beers, ice creams and frozen yoghourt, the list is long. Since childhood, summer memories hold a special part in our hearts and minds. Each phase of life holds a treasure of different kinds of memories, from kindergarten to school, to high school, college, job, family, and so on.

For Jane, it was a high ride of the summer wave during her college years. Her simple, disciplined life was often put to test by her over-enthusiastic friend Anna who always lived in a reel world. Anna's world revolved around Hollywood stars and their lives. One particular actor whom she followed was Mac. She was a diehard fan of Mac and always dreamt of going on a date with him.

On a summer day when they were in the third year of their college, news started making rounds that the famous SG-starrer movie shoot was happening in a premium star property. And the actor in the lead role was none other than Mac. This piece of news gave Anna butterflies in her stomach and her heart started pounding against her chest. She knew where she had to go to make this happen in reality.

Anna ran down the corridor and banged at the door of her best friend Jane's room. As Jane opened the door, Anna pushed her aside and flew herself on the bed face down. Jane was used to this type of melodrama. This action meant Anna had something really important to talk about and wanted unconditional support from Jane as always.

Jane said, "Anna, out with it. No melodrama, come straight to the point." Anna turned her face sideways, pulled her hair lock behind her ear and flashed an annoying smile. Slowly she got up and said, "You look beautiful today. What a lovely day to go out!" Jane smiled and reached for her book and sat on her chair to study. Anna jumped out of bed and came down on her knees in a puppy pose in front of Jane to catch her attention. Jane knew it was time to let the cat out of the bag. She pulled up Anna and they both sat on the bed.

After a silence that seemed like an eternity, Anna finally spoke, "Look, Jane, I was planning to take you for breakfast in the five-star hotels in our city tomorrow." Jane looked at her in surprise and asked, "Any special occasion! As far as I can remember your birthday is next month. What's so special about tomorrow?"

'Well, tomorrow is special, because Mac is staying in that hotel for his upcoming movie shoot under the SG banner," replied Anna. Jane now understood Anna's childish behaviour. She added, "Let's check out with the hotel people first to confirm." Nodding in agreement, Anna followed Jane out of her room to the phone booth.

After searching in the telephone directory, they were able to find the reception number. Jane dialled and could hear the click of the receiver being picked up. A voice came from another end, "Hello, good morning this is XYZ hotel reception, how may I help you?" Jane replied, "I am a school friend of Mac's, please put me through his room number." The receptionist politely replied, "We don't have any Mr Mac or any crew of the SG-starrer staying in our hotel, maybe you got the wrong hotel. Thank you." And the line got cut. Jane immediately came to know that the receptionist was lying as she had enquired about Mac and the receptionist had added SG's name in the reply. With this confirmation that the Hollywood stars were staying in the hotel, both decided to take the call.

Anna could not sleep well through the night. She kept tossing in her bed and started imagining her meeting with

Mac, world-famous Hollywood star who was everyone's heartthrob. Finally, she went to Jane's room in the wee hours of the morning and slept on the mattress next to her bed. When she opened her eyes, she saw Jane leaning over her with a cappuccino in one hand, smiling as she said, "So, Anna did you meet Mac in your dreams? It's half past eight, drink your coffee and get ready. We should leave by nine." Anna jumped up and ran to her room. In a flashing twenty minutes or less, she was at Jane's door all dressed up for the breakfast at the hotel.

Both of them emptied all their secret pockets and counted the cash in hand. After calculating, they were confident that they had enough for the day. Jane was dressed in simple yet elegant attire, true to her natural self. On the other hand, Anna was all flashy and loud as per her style. They went by public transport to the last but one mile of the hotel to save money. From this point, they hired a cab for the last leg of the journey.

They had decided that they will not enquire at the reception and rather do their own search. They went, explored around and finally decided to sit in the lounge area. From here, they could keep an eye on the reception, lift, restaurant and the main entrance to the hotel. Jane ordered coffee and grilled sandwiches. An hour passed, and there seemed to be no active movement in the hotel.

Anna grew impatient and decided to enquire at the reception. Jane tried to reason out with Anna to be more patient but did not succeed. Suddenly, Jane spotted a famous cinematographer and confirmed her suspicion about the shooting going on in the hotel. Anna, being impatient, could not hold herself back and went to the reception. Jane could see an irritable Anna at the reception. Initially, she seemed confident in her body language, talking with the reception staff. She could see the entire staff nodding their head from left to right in a synchronised manner, which confirmed Jane's suspicion that the SG's entire team was in this hotel.

Jane finished her coffee and walked towards the garden. She saw a bright flash from the corner of her eye. When she turned her head, she could see flashlights, a camera trolley and lots of people at a far distance. She started walking towards that enclosed area with security guards. Meanwhile, Anna returned to her seat to find an empty coffee cup anda half-eaten sandwich, with no clue about Jane. A helper told her that she had seen her friend walking towards the garden. Anna hurriedly walked where the helper had pointed.

Jane requested the security guards for access and she was politely denied. Suddenly, she saw SG in the middle of what seemed like a movie set and screamed her lungs out, "Hey, SG! I am a great fan of yours and I love you." Almost immediately SG moved his head to see who had spoken his name. Jane waved with both her hands. SG signalled the guard to let her in. An escort came to help Jane through and she was guided to a side chair.SG walked towards her with a broad smile and remarked, "Hey girl, what brings you here? Are you really a big fan? I am not used to girls shouting my name. All I hear is Mac, Mac, Mac...."

Jane was an intelligent girl and she meant what she had said. She told him about all his movies, his directorial debut, his first production, etc. SG seemed convinced and happy. "Finally, I have a girl fan base, I am feeling lucky," SG gave one of his most warm heart-touching smiles. He invited Jane to join him to catch glimpses of behind-the-scenes part. On sensing Jane's reluctance, SG said, "Don't worry, you are safe with me. I am not aware of how the media portrays me, believe me, I am a nice man." Jane felt embarrassed and replied, "Oh! I apologise for my reaction. Actually, my friend has come with me and I cannot find her now. She had planned to visit this hotel for breakfast. She is a great fan of Mac and wanted to meet the man of her dreams." SG cut her short and said, "Now I see the whole picture clearly. This was your plan to impress me by claiming to be my fan and get entry into my sets so that your friend could meet her hero. What a great friendship story! I can make my next movie on this script."

Jane apologised once again and made a move to leave. SG once again stopped her and asked her to sit with him. He then summoned one of his spot boys and instructed him to go fetch Anna. Soon, Anna joined them. Sensing a nervous vibe, SG smiled and said, "Let me make things better for all of us. Come on girls, join me for high tea. I will invite Mac also." He started walking and signalled them to follow him. Excitedly, Anna walked ahead with

Jane walking thoughtfully behind her. They sat at a table with four chairs. Soon Mac joined them. Greetings were exchanged. They started sipping their tea. There was pin drop silence.

SG asked routine questions about their college, their parents, aims and ambition. Then he assumed a thoughtful pose. "Have you ever thought about acting in movies Jo? I am taking the liberty of calling you Jo and not Jane," SG asked her. Jane was taken aback by this unusual question and she politely refused. SG reinforced and said, "You should try for auditions for my next project." He then made a square space with both hands, as if holding an imaginary camera and started eyeing Jane through it. "Your profile is perfect. I am sure you will create a sensation. Think about it. You have another six months. My current project will take three months. Then, I will take a three month break before starting my next project. Think about it. Discuss with your family too."

Jane felt uncomfortable and felt as if SG's eyes were piercing through her skin. She didn't realise Anna and Mac were sitting there too. All she could see was SG. Their eyes locked for a brief moment and immediately Jane diverted her attention. Jane could feel a strange sensation within her heart as if her heart skipped a beat. Mac cracked a joke to ease the tension.

Once tea was over Jane thanked them and was about to leave when SG said, "Jo, come with me, I will show you how a movie is made. Bring your friend too." Soon, it was "Jo", "Jo" everywhere. Jane felt uncomfortable with the attention she was getting. Almost everyone knew SG had only one name on his lips.

Anna felt very happy with all the attention she was getting because of her friend. She managed to get a few autographs and was in her happy space. Jane was working on a strategy to leave the hotel. On the pretext of going to the restroom, she started walking towards the exit gate with Anna following her. As she walked, she could hear footsteps behind her. Jane started walking faster and so did the footsteps. "Madam, please slow down. SG Sir is waiting for you and your friend for lunch. I have come to escort you. Please stop." Immediately, Jane slowed down her pace and looked behind. She saw a spot boy panting and signalling her to stop. They went with him. He took them to level twenty, to SG's Presidential Suite. Jane felt uneasy and as soon as she opened the door, she saw the entire crew members eating lunch with SG and Mac. SG waved and called them near him and said, "Help yourself to a sumptuous meal. Don't be surprised by our lunch. Since we travel a lot and do outdoor shoots, our food is cooked by our chef. It comprises boiled rice, boiled pulses, salads and stir-fried vegetables."

Jane and Anna were taken back by the simplicity of the entire team. Mac looked like a boy next door eating a simple meal. Anna's dreamy bubble deflated and she felt heartbroken. Filmmaking was the highest form of creative art where even an ordinary person looked like a superman and women looked like angels, all thanks to makeup, lighting and other effects. Anna ate food in stony silence and in between sneaked a look at Mac. She inched herself towards him and sat beside him. This moment of eating lunch with the man of her dreams was a magical moment that she soaked inside her. Meanwhile, Jane was getting sceptical about SG's behaviour. He had no intention of leaving Jo's side. They spoke on various topics. They seemed to share a very comfortable understanding between both of them. He understood her silence too. Their chemistry was obvious.

As it is, they had started lunch very late, so it was almost evening, by the time lunch was winded up. As if SG read Jane's mind, he commented, "Don't worry, my chauffeur will drop you and your friend at your hostel. I know you won't get a conveyance at this hour from this place. Enjoy the last part of the shoot for the day, have dinner and then I promise I will drop you and your friend safely at your hostel. It's a gentleman's promise." Evening faded, dinner was eaten and after bidding goodbyes and exchange of thanks, Jane sat in his limousine. She felt shaky and disturbed. On the other hand, Anna seemed to be enjoying every moment.

As the chauffeur started the ignition, SG signalled him to open the front door. He sat inside and turned towards Jane and said, "Will you do me two favours." "Depends upon the kind of favours," Jane replied. He gave a short laugh and said, "One is you will reconsider your decision about being a part of my next project and the second is you will drop me at the airport when I leave your city in a week." Jane nodded in affirmation and he got down and told the driver to drop them safely at their hostel. Sky Gods had other plans. It rained heavily at night. There was water logging everywhere with a complete blackout. Jane and Anna got scared as they were with an unknown chauffer and could not assess the place where they were stuck in the water. Luckily, the chauffeur knew the ways of the city and managed to drop them safely at their hostel gate.

Jane and Anna went to their rooms and slept. The day seemed like a mystery and too weird to be true. The next morning when they woke up, they pinched themselves to reality. And yes, the day that went by had happened in reality. When they went to the mess room for their breakfast, they felt other girls looking at them curiously and suspiciously. Few were smiling and few were whispering. Finally, one girl, who was known for bullying spoke, "So, how was your night? We came to know you were dropped off in a limousine which had a big sticker of SG, seems like you had a great night!" And her group broke into loud laughter. Anna told Jane to ignore them. They got dressed up for college.

The news that plain Jane and her friend Anna had been dropped at the hostel in a car owned by the giant of Hollywood, SG had already spread like a wildfire. The only confusion that prevailed was which one of them had caught the fancy of SG. There were bets on the names of Jane and Anna. Ignoring everyone, they tried to focus on their classes but could not bear the looks of everyone.

After attending for half a day, they came back to their rooms. That one day had created a huge wave in their lives and they didn't know what to do.

Jane buried her head under the pillow and was about to sleep when the watchman knocked on her door and informed her that her close friend was on the line and wanted to speak to her. Jane went and as soon as she pulled the receiver to her ear, she knew it was SG's call. She could hear his breath as if he was breathing down her neck. He spoke, "Hello Jo, I just wanted to check about your well-being. Last night it poured heavily and there was water logging and a blackout. Hope my chauffer did his duty responsibly." Jane nodded and didn't utter a word. SG said, "What happened? Why are you sounding low?" Jane didn't want to share anything yet she found herself pouring her heart out to him. He listened patiently and waited for her to complete. Then taking a moment he said, "Listen, Jo, all these girls who are bullying you, are actually jealous of you. You are not aware that girls go to any extent to be friends with me, especially when I offer them a role. You are naïve and very pure. This is what attracted me to you. I will take care of things. Don't worry." The phone line got disconnected.

There was no communication from SG for the next few days. Gradually things settled down. Jane wanted to forget about this episode. Anna on the other hand had appeared to mature since that day and sounded more focused and disciplined. She removed posters of Mac from her wardrobe and replaced all showbiz magazines with her study books.

Almost a week had passed since the SG episode. Jane was combing her hair when she heard the security guard knock on her door. "Jane madam, a car is waiting for you outside the hostel gate. Kindly come and check it out," the security guard spoke and left. Jane knew it must be SG's car and he must be on his way to the airport. She suddenly felt emotionally weak and tears rolled down her eyes.

She just could not understand the emotions she was undergoing through. One part of her wanted her life to be as it was before she had met SG and the other half yearned for SG's company. She wore casual denim and a white T-shirt. Grabbing her shades and tying her sneakers, she locked her room. She walked confidently through the hostel gate. The chauffer recognised her and opened the door. She sat inside and saw she was all alone. Sensing her uneasiness, the chauffeur said, "Madam, SG Sir is waiting for you at the airport. He has a flight in the next couple of hours."

Jane could see the hostel girls peeping out of their room windows and waving at her, a few of them winked and blew kisses. Some shouted, "Jane, do agree to SG's proposal. Go girl go take the plunge, ride the summer wave." Jane felt as if she was back to her original self and felt relieved. As they reached the airport, she saw SG with his crew. He had wrapped up his shoot and was heading back home. He smiled and waved at her. "Jo, how are you? I know something has happened to both of us, some unknown chemistry that even I am unable to understand. You are half my age and I just cannot stop thinking about you. I have depleted all my energy in restraining myself from calling or seeing you. But today, I had to see you one more time before I left. In case you change your mind, give me a call." He handed her his card. He asked for her permission to hug and she agreed. They both hugged.

Their embrace symbolised a perfect moment, a union of two divine souls. Time stood frozen. They were not willing to let go of each other. Jane felt a heavy load had lifted off her chest. They smiled and he left without looking back. She held his card and cherished his touch. The entire crew entered the airport premises and Jane just stood there waiting. She felt a tap on her shoulder, "Madam, I am getting late. SG Sir had asked me to drop you back at your hostel. I have another ride booked for today." The chauffeur spoke. Jane jilted out of her dream into reality.

On her way back to the hostel, she started reconsidering her decision and by the time she approached her hostel gate, she knew in her heart what she wanted. She requested the driver to drop her back at the airport. He agreed. The ride back must have taken more than an hour or so. As they made their way to the airport road, she could see fire and fumes in the sky with the sound of screeching police cars and ambulance sirens wailing. The place where she had stood and hugged SG was now crowded with police and paramedic staff. She feared the worst.

She left the limousine and walked towards the airport. On enquiring with the police, she came to know that the flight in which SG and his entire crew were had caught fire in two of its engines and had to land in an emergency as soon as it took off the runway. There was no clue about survivors as rescue work was going on. Frantically, she went inside to the runway despite police and security holding her back and advising her not to go. Another one of the engines had caught fire and there was a danger of an explosion in the rear end of the aircraft.

Where there is a will, there is a way. Jane could identify SG in the debris by the ring on his middle finger. She shouted for help and managed to dig out SG. Looking at her SG managed to smile weakly and said, "My Jo, I knew you would change your mind. I love you. Do you feel the same for me?" As he uttered his last word, his hand dropped. Before Jo could say, "I do" SG had left his mortal coil for a higher journey. Jane hugged him tight and rocked his body in her lap. She had been touched by true love this summer. But it didn't last long enough for her to reciprocate.

Fast forward twenty years, Jane is an entrepreneur with a family, happily married and has managed to move ahead in her life. Still, the thought of SG stirs a whirlpool of emotions in her and she vividly feels his touch and smell.

Whenever these emotions weigh on her, Jane looks up at the vast sky and gently utters " Ciao, Amor Mio! *Goodbye my love.*"

27

MY CYCLE

Ticket to Freedom

I cannot think of concluding my book without a note on my favourite mode of transport, my cycle. Driving since the age of sixteen, my love for four-wheelers is in a declining phase.

Living in a small city where distances are less, I always yearned to cycle to work. I am leaving aside all the discussions and reasons. Finally, almost three years ago, I gifted myself a Tata bicycle, a non-gear one. I have immense respect for the Tata Group, as I am an alumnus of TMH, Mumbai too. Their philosophy is very genuine. They believe money always changes hands, we are just carriers. If one is financially sound, one should pay back to society.

When I ride my cycle to my workplace through the roads of my city, I feel teleported into another world. The cool wind brushes my cheek and gently caresses my hair. Everything seems so beautiful and serene. One feels connected with Mother Earth as the guilt of pollution is absolved. This mode is eco-friendly besides being cost-effective.

The experience is just like being in love. Whatsoever may be the mindset or the challenges I face in day-to-day life, once I sit on the seat and start paddling, all worries seem to vanish into thin air. This is one of the best anti-stress therapies, just like a walk in a garden or meditation.

No worry about traffic jams or roadblocks, one can just lift the cycle and move ahead. There are many cons too as the majority of Indian roads do not have a cycling track. Another drawback is being bullied by other two-wheelers or four-wheelers, who purposely honk loudly or breeze past at high speeds to scare the cyclist. Such kinds of incidents do not bother a person who is in love. For everything is fair in love.

Whatever may be the stressful situation at home or the workplace, once we meet and I ride, all the stress bubbles burst and what remains is a big smile on my face! I recommend cycle therapy to everyone, especially school children and women. Try it! I bet you will bless me.

It's time to meet my love.

28

I AM IN LOVE!

Gratitude in Abundance

This is a positive reaffirmation that everyone must make every day starting with:

I am in love with myself.

I am in love with life

I am in love with my family.

I am in love with my profession.

I am in love with my friends.

I am in love with my yoga/cycling.

I am in love with my fitness/gym.

I am in love with my neighbour.

I am in love with mankind.

I am in love with nature.

I am in love with my city.

I am in love with my country.

I am in love with birds.

I am in love with plants.

I am in love with animals.

The list is endless.

A heart filled with love and a soul filled with gratitude is all that is needed for this world to be a happier, peaceful place,

Such positive affirmations help us stay motivated and keep us in a positive frame of mind.

Let's start each day with a heart full of gratitude and on a humble note, "I am in love with God," and add on to the list of I am in love.

Dr. Reemanshu Bansal (pen name Juju's Pearls) hails from New Delhi, India. Currently, she is based in Punjab, India. She is a blogger, writer, social activist, traveller, counsellor and a doctor (Radiologist) by profession. She has done schooling from Cambridge School, New Delhi, medical school in Bengaluru and Internship training in New Delhi. Her selection to Tata Memorial Hospital, Mumbai for Residency in Radio-Diagnosis was the turning point in her life. She set out on a journey to find a solution for freedom from grief. She learnt that a 'listening ear' was the key to other people's hearts.

She is a dedicated professional and has an all-female staff centre. She has adopted forty families in the slums and runs an evening school for their children. She regularly takes part in walking challenges. Being a Greenpeace Initiative crusader, she has adopted the bicycle as a way of life. She is a WWF volunteer and adopts trees as birthday gifts for her near and dear ones. For her overall health, she does regular meditation and yoga.

Her family has travelled across India and abroad. She believes travelling to places and experiencing different cultures is like a wonder drug for children. This is real teaching, which leaves a mark on a child's mind. Family times and vacations help in confidence and personality building besides bonding. She practises the mantra of 'Simple living, high thinking' as taught to her by her mother.

Her personal blog (**reemanshu.blogspot.com**) has readers across the globe. Tea-time at her workplace has evolved into counselling and therapeutic sessions. She loves to share her life experiences in her own style statement under the pen name **"Juju's Pearls"**. Her first book, *Momsie Popsie Diary Tea-Time Chit-chat on Living Life*, ranked **Amazon#2 as the best hot new seller**. It is available as paperback and e-Book on all e-commerce sites in the Indian and international market.

Her readers compare her work to Ruskin Bond, Robin Sharma, Chetan Bhagat and Sudha Murthy. She has authored ten books, two as a single author and eight as a co-author. Some of them are *#Verses of Love, Love Me, Till Your Cessation!, My Feelings on Paper –Book 1 of My Heart Goes On, Wide Awake Volume 1, How I Calibrate My Life!, The Kolkata Diaries – Volume II, Summer Waves Volume II, Stories from India Volume I*. She has conceptualised her third book too which will be a novel series. This book is very close to heart as it encompasses various kinds of love. This book has been inked with her soul.

Catch her latest brews from, Mind's Café–**reemanshu. blogspot.com**

Follow her Insta handle: reemanshubansal

Join her **Facebook Page: Juju,s Reader Club**

For any queries, reemanshu2003@gmail.com

MESSAGE TO GEN-NEXT

If one does what one likes then the work becomes a hobby and life becomes a picnic. Life is all about self-discipline, introspection and remaining focused. A self-motivated person always inspires others. There is no other magic way. Always "Aspire to Inspire". Your life is an inspiration to many.

My message, especially to youngsters is—Live every moment as life is happening NOW. Each moment lived is to be cherished. Be a learner and a seeker as life happens only once. Keep yourself a priority besides your work and keep time for your hobbies too.

Follow your heart but remember to take your brain along. Focus on your education and career. Love can wait. There is a right time to do everything in life. Student life should focus on education, overall development and career.

A life lived in a fully conscious, aware state, is the most powerful addiction.

Get addicted to this.

EPILOGUE

"Verba volant, scripta manent"

(Latin proverb meaning "Spoken words fly away,
written words remain.")

Love is one emotion, which everyone has in abundance. To love and to be loved is the main goal. Any relationship or work soars higher if there is love. Some are born expressive, for others, they need to learn. This emotion is a perfect balm for hurting wounds and acts like a tranquilliser for soothing nerves.

Love is multi-dimensional. It cannot be calibrated or defined. It is limitless, boundless and infinite. Let's express our love with an open heart and outstretched welcoming arms. If these stories touch a chord or you resonate with this book, please express love to your loved ones more often.

Carpe diem! (Seize the day)

Donec iterum conveniant! (Till we meet again)

AUTHOR'S AWARDS

1. Winner of 'Literary awards 2022 Non-fiction-Best Biographies/Memoirs'

2. Awardee 'Emerging Author of the year 2022'

3. Awardee 'India Prime Top 100 Authors 2022'

4. Tagore Commemorative Honouree Author for 2022 for Literary Excellence and beyond

5. Recipient of 'India Star Inspiring Woman of the year 2022 (all-rounder)'

6. 'Sahityakosh Samman' for literary work recognition

7. Literary Award, LITFEST 22

8. Awardee Book Honour, World Book Day

9. Awardee 'Certificate of Excellence', Tagore Commemorative Edition, 2022

10. Awardee Category 'India 50 Inspiring Women 2022'

11. Awardee 'Outstanding influencer of the year'

12. Awardee 'Inspiring Indians 2022'

13. Awardee 'Excellence in writing beyond medical field'

14. Fellowship Certificate, Inspiring Indians 2022

15. Book in 'Must read shelf' at LIFEST 22

16. Coverage in Litteratura magazine (April'22, July'22).

17. Nominated for 'NDWBF 22 – New Delhi World Book Fair'

18. Nominated for 'Bharat Gaurav Shree Sammaan'

19. Nominated for 'Reader's Choice Awards 2022' by TCK Publishing, USA

Keep loving, keep caring
Keep reading, keep sharing